TO TAUNT A WOUNDED TIGER

A novel by

Anthony Bruce

To Clara, with best wishes, [signature]

GLENDAMBO BOOKS

Copyright © 1997 Anthony Bruce

Canadian Cataloguing in Publication Data

Bruce, Anthony Alexander, 1939-
To taunt a wounded tiger

First Printing 1997
Second Printing 2005, revised

ISBN 0-9681787-0-7
I. Title.
PS8553.R72T62 1997   C813'.54   C97-910062-3
PR9199.3.B73T62 1997

A Glendambo Book

Published By: Glendambo Publishing
151 Saltair Lane
Saltspring Island
BC V8K 1Y5. Canada

Cover Design by: Irwan Kurnaedy: Irwan Kurnaedy Design
Layout and Typesetting by Glendambo Publishing

Printed in Canada

For: ELENA KATERINA MIA

With grateful thanks:

In Canada, to:
George and Barbara
Kathleen
Win
Dr Anthony Jenkins
Laura and Brian
Irwan
RCMP - Victoria/Ganges

In Britain, to:
Lady Gloria Lawrence
Andy Bruce

"There are three things you should never do," Rafa told Colin. "Never piss into the wind. Never lie, unless it's to comfort the dying, and never, ever, taunt a wounded tiger."

Cast of Characters

David Mornay	Semi-retired mining consultant (ex-Vietnam combat engineer).
Kate Mornay	David Mornay's wife.
Laura Mornay	David and Kate Mornay's daughter (six years old).
Nigel Mornay	David Mornay's brother, Chairman of the Board, Mornay Industries.
Judith Mornay	Nigel's wife.
Colin Mornay	Nigel and Judith's only son, David Mornay's nephew.
Rafa Modesto	Former mercenary pilot, close friend of David and Colin Mornay.
Davis	International terrorist—team leader—hijack strike force.
Kassim	Hamas terrorist—second in command-hijack strike force.
O'Doull	Ex-IRA terrorist—hired by hijack strike force.
Rostov	KGB senior officer. Former head of KGB disinformation—section V.
Capt Strydom	747 Captain—South African Airways.
Dar Yassin	Hamas—deputy chairman—Political.
Ali Khufra	Hamas—field commander—Operations.
Abu Hakim	PLO—deputy chairman—Political.
Hafiz Ahmad	PLO—senior officer—Political.
Professor Watson	United Nations delegate—Middle East expert.
Viktor Kuchinsky	United Nations delegate—Russia.
Michael Monroe	United Nations delegate—Canada.
Ali Al-Azhar	United Nations delegate—Sudan.
Edward Mason	CIA—head of counter-terrorist operations.
Jack Dehenny	CIA—deputy chief of CT operations.
Eli Natan	Mossad—Israeli intelligence operative.
Bob Nichols	RCMP—Inspector—Victoria, B.C.
Jim McUlroy	RCMP—Deputy Commissioner—Ottawa.
Ed Benson	RCMP—Head of Political Security Section—Ottawa.

Prologue.

Kassim snapped the slide on the pistol, pointed at the wall and pulled the trigger. The dry click of the striker echoed around the room. "For fuck's sake will you grow up. Put that bloody toy away." Rostov was irritated and snapped savagely, looking hard at Kassim: "You'll have plenty of opportunities to impress everyone later."

Kassim laughed but put the pistol down on the table. O'Doull leaned forward and stabbed with a thick finger at the opened plan on the coffee table, his brow furrowed. "What makes you so sure that their security is lax? .. overconfidence is a sure recipe for disaster." Rostov turned cold eyes to O'Doull and, for a second, the hardened IRA killer felt a chill run up his spine. Rostov's eyes suddenly warmed: "Good, good . . . caution is the trademark of a professional." Smiling, he tapped the pocket of his Armani suit and, finding his cigarette case, snapped it open. He did not offer a cigarette to O'Doull or to the other three men and one woman sitting around the coffee table. Carefully selecting a gold sobranie filter, he felt his opposite pocket and drew out a monogrammed silver lighter. Nobody moved. They were not accustomed to being treated lightly but, for Rostov, they waited, waited for him to light up and break the silence. Drawing a deep lungful of smoke, he leaned back in the chair.

"I had agents fly Air Canada and other airlines to New York from Vancouver three times last month. They carried in their hand luggage the weapons you will use. Of course they did not show up on the security screen. They are designed not to. Even so, I am unimpressed with security at either Vancouver or Toronto; Canada has not had a hijacking and they're far too casual. However . . ." his voice hardened, "a great deal of planning and effort have gone into this operation so you will follow the plan to the letter. Anyone who believes that he's entitled to a little independent action . . ," he swung his eyes to look at Kassim and paused, " . . . will find he's badly mistaken."

Kassim tried to hold Rostov's gaze but was forced to look away. Like the others he was afraid of the stocky Russian's aura of power. Behind that, a sense of evil followed the man like the whiff of sulphur fumes in still air.

Chapter 1

Victoria - British Columbia, Canada.

Nigel Mornay put down the phone and, smiling, walked to stand in front of the plate-glass window that filled an entire wall of his office situated on the top floor of the Mornay Tower Block, Victoria's highest building. He stood there, musing over the events of the past few years, his back to his luxurious office: an office that befitted the chairman of the board and majority shareholder of the massive conglomerate of companies that comprised Mornay Industries. Nigel looked out at the panorama across the green-grey waters of the Strait of Juan de Fuca to the distant Olympic mountains and smiled to himself as he recalled the just-completed conversation with his son.

"Dad, would you and mom be very disappointed if I didn't come to Cancun with you this summer?"

"Well, that depends. Your mother will be disappointed, of course, but I assume you have a compelling reason. What is she—blonde, brunette or redhead—hmm?"

"Dream on! No, nothing like that. I've had a letter from Rafa and suddenly felt an urge to see him again."

"Go down to Chile?"

"Yes, I thought I might convince Uncle Dave to come and bring Kate and Laura."

"I see . . . I know you missed seeing him last year, but isn't he coming up this way again?"

"Dad, Rafa was here for less than two days last year, and he spent all that time with Dave and Kate on Saltspring. I was in the middle of exams, if you recall. And to answer your question, I don't know if he is planning another trip, but I really feel the need to see him again."

"Hmm, yes . . . yes . . . that's understandable. Well, considering what we all owe Rafa, that's not a bad idea. When do you want to go?"

"There's a couple of weeks left to go until the end of semester, and then I thought I'd spend a week at home with you and mom before you take off to Cancun. I could leave for Chile on that weekend."

"Well, I'm glad you're planning some time at home," Nigel chuckled. "Your mother would have both our guts if you decided to leave right after your last lecture." He paused. "Why not fly with us to Cancun and I'll arrange some business for Dave to take care of in Chile? Mornay mining is looking at some claim properties there. The company jet can drop off your mother and myself at Cancun then fly the three of you on to Santiago, where you can spend a couple of weeks enjoying yourselves."

"Well, that would be great, but I don't want to mooch a ride off the company. I have some money saved, you know." Colin was incredibly stiff-necked when it came to taking advantage of his position as the only son of the most powerful businessman in Western Canada.

"Colin, stop talking rubbish. What the hell's the use of having aircraft if I can't use them. And in any case, I had intended to ask David to fly down with Joel Buchinsky to look at these claims." Joel Buchinsky was Mornay Industries' chief pilot.

"Well, as long as you're sure this is not a special trip." Colin still sounded dubious.

"Colin!" Nigel's voice had a touch of asperity. "I own the company. One day you'll own the company. For heaven's sake stop wearing a hairshirt. I'm all for economy and responsible behaviour, but taking anything to extremes is not only bad, it's stupid."

"Sorry!" Colin was contrite. "It's very generous of you. I'll write to Rafa this evening and speak to Uncle Dave as well."

Colin was in his fourth year in the faculty of engineering at the University of British Columbia in Vancouver. A ruggedly handsome youth, he had developed from a spoilt, wilful and thoroughly unpleasant adolescent into a quiet and thoughtful man.

Nigel's face tightened as he remembered the past and the unruly son Colin had once been. A frightening time when he had feared his son would end up in prison for peddling drugs: eight years ago, Colin, then a mere 15-year-old, had been sent for his own safety to Namibia in Africa to spend time with Nigel's older brother, David. From the moment he had arrived at the hot, sandy, uranium mine of Tsamma Ridge and town of Swakopmund, Colin had clashed with his uncle David, a man he had never met before.

Five years older than Nigel, David had run away to sea at 16 to escape his bullying, sadistic father. For no apparent reason, their father had disliked his first born intensely and made no secret of his feelings. Nigel, the younger son, on the other hand, could do no wrong, and the difference in their ages meant that as children they had spent very little time in each other's company. Only in the last 8 years, since David's semi-retirement after 25 years with ConAmGeo, a major mining company, had a closeness developed between the two men.

As a young teenager, Nigel had tried to gather information on his older brother during those years, but his father forbade all mention of his eldest son. The boy's mother, a frail, gentle person, could neither understand nor deal with the harshness of her husband's attitude and slowly retreated over the years into a cocoon of vagueness and spirituality. Nigel always believed that she had died of a broken heart and, considering his father's usual coldness to his wife's causes, was totally stunned to see his father devastated by her death. The elder Mornay irrationally blamed David.

Nigel sighed, remembering how close he had come to following in the footsteps of his father and losing the love of his own son. True, Colin had been a spoilt, unpleasant brat, but whose fault was that? Looking back, he recalled, with a twinge of guilt, how indifferent he had been to his own wife Judith's pleadings that he spend more time at home. Colin had fallen in with a group of local drug dealers whose agenda, it later transpired, was to incriminate the boy and then blackmail the father. Only through quick action in sending the reluctant youth to stay with David in Namibia did Nigel avert a potential disaster.

"Mr. Mornay." The voice broke his reverie, and he turned to see Sybil Burgess, his executive secretary, at the door. Sybil had been his secretary for the last 15 years. A tall, plain, angular, middle-aged woman who'd never married, she was Nigel's walking encyclopedia on company business. Nigel valued her highly and considered the very generous salary he paid her less than sufficient compensation for her many skills.

"I tried the intercom, but you did not reply."

Nigel smiled: "Sorry, Sybil, I was miles away. Colin just phoned. I was remembering his trip to Tsamma."

Sybil Burgess grimaced; "I would think that was a time best forgotten."

"Come on, Sybil, look what came out of it. We got Colin back, a much better person I might add, and with the added bonus of David and Kate."

Sybil shook her head at the memory. "I don't want to be frightened like that ever again and, talking of Kate, she's on her way up to see you. Security in the lobby have just called."

"Well, well. First Colin, now Kate. This is turning out to be a better morning than I expected."

Sybil grunted. "Don't forget you have a meeting at 11a.m. with the premier, and Herr Shimmel has a conference call set up from Hamburg at 3 p.m." At that moment there was a knock, and his brother's wife stuck her head around the half-open door.

"Sorry to barge in, but the door was open. Are you both very busy?" The accent was English with a softer overlay.

Nigel was always amazed at how his brother had managed to capture this lovely, gentle, clever creature. For someone as hard, cold and aloof as David, it seemed totally incongruous that their marriage was as happy as it obviously was. "Kate!" He held out both hands. "What a wonderful surprise. Come in—come in." He embraced his sister-in-law. "What brings you to town? Is David with you?"

Kate Mornay laughed, a soft throaty chuckle: "Fat chance! You know how he hates the city." She placed several shopping bags on the carpet and stripped off her gloves. "Hullo, Sybil," she kissed the older woman on the cheek. "I'm so sorry, it must be age or something; I don't know how I forgot your birthday last week." Bending, she retrieved a small object wrapped in opaque tissue paper from one of the bags at her feet. "I found this in an antique shop on Fort Street. I know you collect them. Happy belated birthday!" She opened the paper and handed Sybil a small half-round glass paperweight with thin multi-coloured swirls of glass beneath the smooth surface.

Sybil flushed with pleasure. "Well, thank you, it's lovely . . ," she ran her fingers caressingly over the surface, " . . . can I get you both some coffee?"

Nigel raised his eyebrows enquiringly, "Kate?"

"Oh yes, I'd love some . . . but do you have time?"

"I don't have anything desperate until 11 a.m, and nothing would give me greater pleasure than to spend a few minutes with you. By the way, Colin has just phoned."

Sybil turned to leave. "I'll fetch the coffee, and keep the hounds at bay for 10 minutes."

"Thanks, Sybil; come and sit down, Kate." Nigel took his sister-in-law's arm and led her to a deep easy chair in a corner of the vast office. He sat down opposite in a similar chair and smiled at her across the low mahogany coffee table. "Now, let me tell you what Colin is planning. But first, what is David up to? I hardly see him these days."

"Oh, he's gone off with Laura to look at a rotten old tugboat. One of his cronies, who thinks because David is an engineer he is an expert on everything, is thinking of buying it. Poor David! He tried to explain that his expertise is mining, but Bob won't listen. Anyway, they left home before I did. Laura was very excited at the thought of a real tugboat ride. I think the only reason David agreed to the trip was because Laura was so keen."

Nigel chuckled. "She certainly has him wrapped around her little finger. For someone like David, who Rafa says was a pretty hard taskmaster in his construction days, it's quite a transformation."

"I know. I spend half my time holding him back. He'd spoil her rotten if I didn't stop him. Fortunately, she seems to have inherited his lack of desire for material goods. I'm sure she lets him get things sometimes, not because she wants them but because she knows it gives him pleasure." Kate reached up and, removing a silk headband, shook her head to loosen the honey-coloured mane of hair that fell to her shoulders. "You said Colin had phoned. How is he? I was thinking of persuading David to take me over to Vancouver to see the Bolshoi ballet and see Colin at the same time."

"Well, Colin wants to duck out of the trip to Cancun and visit Rafa in Santiago instead. He intends to ask both of you to join him. Laura as well, of course. He'll be phoning David tonight to sound you out."

"Oh, poor Judith, she'll be very disappoint . . ." Kate protested.

"Wait . . . wait." Nigel held up his hands, smiling. "Colin will spend a week at home with Judith and me before we leave. She understands the bond Colin has with Rafa. So the plan is that we'll all fly down to Cancun in the jet, then the four of you will fly on to Santiago. I want David to look at some claims in the Cerro de Olivares region, but that will only take a day or two and, for the rest of the time, you can have a vacation. Do you think you can persuade that husband of yours to leave his island?"

Kate laughed. "For something like this I won't have to push very hard. It's only when I try to get him to a show in Victoria or Vancouver that I have to sulk."

Just then Sybil returned with a tray on which sat a silver thermos jug of fresh coffee, milk and sugar in silver containers, and two china coffee cups. She placed the tray on the table between them, and, while Kate helped Sybil remove the items from the tray, Nigel studied his sister-in-law. She was lovely, that was a given, but hers was a classical, ageless beauty that would have men turning to look when she reached 60 and beyond. He had never heard her say or do anything unkind, and strength of character was reflected in the strong lines of her jaw. This was no lightweight, pretty fluffhead. Kate had graduated with an honours degree in chemistry from South Africa's top university, married a classmate, and moved with her then-husband to the

Tsamma Uranium Mine in Namibia where she met his brother David.

Nigel marvelled at the events that had led to their falling in love. Her marriage to an ambitious, upwardly mobile financial whiz kid had been in crisis even before she met David. Kate had fought hard against falling in love with him, despite being strongly attracted to the quiet construction boss. Only when he'd been seriously injured in an accident had she realised that she could not give up the lonely, grim man who seemed to have had more than his fair share of sadness. It was at that time when Colin, hating his father, his uncle, and his enforced sojourn in Namibia, had been lost in the desert. Rafa Modesto, an ex-mercenary pilot and adventurer, was then working for the Tsamma Uranium Company. The pilot, David Mornay's closest friend, had developed an unlikely affection for the spoilt, arrogant youth and was teaching Colin the rudiments of flying while, at the same time, trying to mediate between the uncle and nephew. When Colin had been lost, a massive search was initiated, and Rafa, David and Kate had been instrumental in finding him.

Two men died in that search, Nigel thought somberly: one, another friend of David's, and the other, the driver of the tour bus. The events of that terrible time changed Colin, peeling away his immaturities and selfishness, and he'd formed a very strong bond with David and Rafa. Returning to Canada, he plunged into his studies with a dedication that surprised and pleased his father. After completing high school, he'd spent a year working, as a volunteer, for an aid agency in Central Africa before returning to start university in Vancouver.

"Nigel." Kate placed the coffee cup in front of him as Sybil made for the door.

"What? . . . Oh sorry, I was miles away."

"Always the business tycoon. Why don't you take more time out? Come to Saltspring for the weekend. You know we'd love to have you and Judith." Kate raised her cup and took a sip.

He looked into the smoky grey-green eyes and his face lightened. "We'd enjoy that, but I have to be in Bangkok at the weekend. Actually, I was thinking about Colin and the time he was lost in the Namib."

"Don't," Kate shivered. "Sometimes when I'm feeling low, I think how differently everything might have turned out. All I can say is, thank God for Rafa; he was a rock all through those days."

"Yes, that's why I'm glad Colin feels the need to see Rafa again. Changing the subject, how are your parents?" Trish and Jack 'Scottie' Scott, Kate's parents, had retired to South Africa from their farm in Kenya 20 years before. Once a year David, Kate and Laura made the long trip from Western Canada to Johannesburg to spend a month there.

"Slowing down, but Scottie still refuses to accept that he's nearly 70 years old." She smiled ruefully. "He claims he'll be around for Laura's wedding. His doctor keeps telling him to take things easy, but that's so much water off a duck's back. David's like an old hen, every time we visit; he keeps telling me and mom to make Scottie slow down."

"You can't convince them to resettle over here?"

"No. Scottie's the genuine article, a real old Africa hand; he would be miserable anywhere else. Even the rise in violence over the last two years doesn't seem to worry him."

"But you worry, don't you? They're so far away."

"Of course I do, but then I worry when David goes off on one of his trips. One has to learn to live with fears. Don't tell me that you weren't worried all the time Colin was working for AfriAid."

"Touché. . . ." Nigel sighed. "I only want you to know that I would be very willing to help them with immigration or anything else they could need."

Kate touched his hand. "I know you would, and thank you, but don't think that David and I haven't tried over the years. Scottie and mom do not want to live anywhere else, but . . ." she spread her hands expressively, "I live in hope, and we'll keep trying."

At that moment Sybil looked around the door. "The premier's

office has just phoned. Can they move the meeting up to 10.30 a.m? I said you were in conference but that I would call back in a few minutes."

"Damn! Yes, call them back and say I'll be there. Call George and tell him to stand by." Nigel stood. "Kate, I'm sorry, but this is very important . . . forgive me?"

"Of course." She leant forward and finished the last of her coffee before rising. "I was very lucky as it was to catch you at a slack moment." She smiled. "You'll have to visit the farm soon. David keeps grumbling that you're hardly ever in Canada these days, and Laura misses Colin a lot."

"OK, that's a promise. Which car are you driving?"

"My little Neon, why?"

"I wish you'd let George pick you up at the ferry or drive something more solid, like David's 4x4. I worry about those little cars; there's no real strength in them."

Kate laughed as she pulled her coat on. "Now you sound just like David. I love my little bug and don't want a bigger car?"

Nigel shook his head. "Women, I'll never understand them!" He walked with Kate to his private elevator and, giving her a final hug, turned to collect the briefcase that Sybil was holding. "I'll call Dave tonight. Perhaps I can arrange my schedule to have a few days on Saltspring. You know, I still wish David would agree to join the board. I keep hoping time and your influence will erase those bad memories of his childhood and Vietnam."

Kate shook her head; "He likes things as they are. He doesn't have those terrible nightmares any more, but he still won't talk about the past to anyone but Rafa. When Rafa was visiting last year they sat up talking all hours of the night. But David's so much more relaxed and enjoys those trips you send him on. He says the 5 percent share of Mornay Industries you forced your father to leave him in the will is enough money for ten lifetimes."

"Oh, it's not the money! You know that. Hell, even without his inheritance, you're very comfortably off. He never spent anything on himself in all those years with ConAmGeo, and Addison has made some very astute investments on his behalf."

Addison was the chief financial officer for Mornay Industries. "But I need him. His international experience would be of enormous value to the company. Work on him for me—truly, you'd be doing me a huge favour."

"Nigel, as you well know, I love David far too much to try and influence him against his best instincts." She smiled at his grimace—"Come now, we have this discussion at least once a year"—and kissed his cheek. "Go and see your premier, Mr. Tycoon. I'm off back to my bucolic haven."

Nigel shook his head ruefully, "Ok—Ok." He waved as the elevator doors closed soundlessly.

Chapter 2

Santiago - Chile

Again the phone tinkled softly. The man, awake now, reached over the woman lying beside him and lifted the receiver.

"Si?"

"Rafa, is that you?"

"Dave? . . . Dave! . . Hold on. Let me get to a place where we can talk." Fully awake now, the man slid out of bed and, naked, carried the cordless phone into the next room away from the sleeping woman. The ridged scars on his stocky, muscled frame stood out like braided rope on the swarthy skin of his back and chest. "What is it, amigo . . . what's up?"

"Kate is dead . . . my Kate is dead . . ." The agony in the caller's voice flooded into the quiet room, and, for a moment, the naked man swayed, reaching out to steady himself against the sofa back.

"O Dios mio! . . . Oh no, sweet Jesus, no . . . Don't tell me that . . . How? . . . When?"

"This afternoon . . ." The caller drew a deep shuddering breath and then continued. "I've just come back from the hospital. Kate went into Victoria this morning . . . Oh dear God, Rafa, for nothing important . . . She just wanted to get a few things to brighten up Laura's room, nothing really important. A young punk in a pickup ran a red light and broadsided her little car." The caller's voice rose suddenly in bitter anger. "Drunk . . . The son-of-a-bitch was drunk . . . drunk Rafa, at noon!" There was a silence broken only by the sound of hoarse gasping as the caller struggled to regain his composure. "Kate . . . my lovely Kate . . . she died in the ambulance."

Rafa Modesto sagged. More than anyone in the world he knew how much David Mornay adored his wife.

"Oh, my friend . . ." he started, and his voice broke. "I'm so sorry, Dave. My friend . . . I will come . . ." He squinted at the ornate clock over the mantlepiece. "I'll catch the first flight in the morning, but I'll take most of the day to get to you . . . Are you going to be OK? . . . Is Nigel or Colin there?"

"Colin? . . . Colin . . . is coming . . .he's still at university . . . Nigel has called UBC; Colin's coming tonight . . . Rafa, come quickly . . ." Rafa could hear a muffled conversation then another familiar voice came on the line.

"Rafa, it's Nigel Mornay speaking. David is spending the night here at my house. I thought of sending the company plane to fetch you but it won't save any time. Do you need me to arrange your flight from this end?"

"No . . . no, I'll take the LanChile flight that leaves at seven. . . How is he, Nigel?"

"In shock . . . as we all are. The doctor has given him a powerful sedative. We're very worried, Rafa. He doesn't seem to be here— you know what I mean? He appears disconnected, above all of this . . . Rafa, I love my brother, but I can't get through to him. Next to Kate and Laura, you're the closest person to him, and we need you now. Thank you for coming."

"Of course, of course I must come. He is my friend, you know that . . . Nigel, watch Colin carefully too. Your son adored Kate, and this will be as hard on him as on Dave. I will call you with my flight times and see you tomorrow night. Goodnight, Nigel." Rafa Modesto put down the phone slowly, then his powerful shoulders bowed and, cradling his head, he began to weep.

At last it was over. The cold wind blowing up the long reach into Fulford Harbour flattened the grass in the churchyard and whipped the priest's cassock and surplice around his ankles before moving on up the valley to batter the ancient diorite walls of Mount Maxwell. A hand touched his elbow.

"Come on, Dave; it's time to go."

He turned slowly, like a man sleepwalking. "No, Rafa . . . Please go. I'll come later . . . I want to spend some time here on my own."

The main group of mourners was leaving, faces down turned. He heard someone sobbing softly into a handkerchief. Nodding gravely to those who had come to comfort, he felt saddened by their hesitance to touch him, knowing that it was his own fault for the image of coldness he projected.

Rafa scanned David Mornay's face anxiously, then nodded with a sigh: "As you wish, amigo. I will wait in the car on the other side of the road."

Mornay squeezed Rafa's arm in a quick gesture of gratitude; "Keep your eye on Colin; he's reaching his limit." Rafa turned to look for David Mornay's nephew and spotted the young man standing apart from the small group that included his parents. Colin, dressed in a charcoal grey suit, white shirt and dark tie had both arms wrapped around his body as if warding off the chill. But it was his posture that alarmed Rafa. Colin stood hunched, diminishing his six-foot height, his taut jaw muscles expressing unbearable tension.

Rafa walked over to where Colin stood and gently, for the young man had not looked up, shook his shoulder. "Colin, you must let her go. She would not want this from you . . . You know that."

"Rafa . . . I don't . . ." The youth looked up and Rafa saw tears tracking down his face. "I can't believe . . ." He raised both hands to his face and his shoulders shook as he tried not to sob. Rafa wrapped his arms around Colin, pulling him close.

"Easy, my friend . . . easy. Dave and little Laura will need us both, more than ever. For them we must be strong." He pushed the youth back, holding the broad shoulders in an iron grip. "Come, walk with me; we'll wait in Dave's car . . . come." Colin's head jerked, then he straightened and, reaching for a handkerchief, blew his nose noisily.

"I'm OK. Thanks, Rafa." He drew in a long breath. "I'll get Laura: she's over there with mom and dad. I don't think she fully understands what has happened; she's so quiet." He stopped, his face working as he tried to control his grief: ". . . oh shit Rafa, what are we going to do? . . . What are we going to do?"

"Keep going, my friend . . . just keep going. The others are depending on us. As for Laura . . . she understands . . . ah yes . . . even a six-year-old understands what losing a mother is. We must be very careful with her. You are her big cousin; she adores you, and it's going to be your strength she will need in the days to come. Dave is retreating into himself. If that drunk had not been killed in the accident, Dave would have surely killed him. That is how far he is from his usual self. When I arrived he was . . ." Rafa grimaced as if in pain, then firmly, " . . . he was not himself, you understand, and he'll be a long time healing."

Colin shivered, then stood taller, the wind-dried tears on his face leaving faint marks down both cheeks.

Victoria

Day 1   0800hrs

Three weeks later:

"You have the tickets? . . . Colin, you have her passport." David Mornay patted his pockets distractedly. "I think you have everything. Now, Laura, you do what Colin tells you . . . OK?" The big man knelt down, holding his arms out to the six-year-old girl who was standing quietly holding a small suitcase and a large teddy bear. "Give me a kiss, my love, and I'll see you soon. You tell Grandpa Scott that Rafa and I will be joining you and Colin in two weeks." The child did not smile and her gaze did not waver from David Mornay's face.

"You will come, won't you daddy?"

David Mornay sighed and wrapped his arms around his daughter. "Of course, my love; I promise. It won't be long. But until Rafa and I get there, Colin will look after you." He tightened his embrace. "You are my starlight; you know that . . . It won't be long; I promise."

Rafa Modesto squatted alongside David Mornay. "I'll make sure he comes, Laura. Now I need a hug as well." Laura Mornay released her father and tightened her little arms around the swarthy Chilean's neck. Looking into the dark eyes, she nodded.

"Mommy said you always keep your promises."

Rafa stroked her honey-gold hair gently and smiled. "From the day you were born, little one, you have been my lady. We'll join you when your father has had his operation." Disentangling himself, he stood and, turning Laura around, his hands resting lightly on the child's shoulders, faced Colin. "You take good care of her, Colin; not too much ice cream, you hear?"

Colin Mornay grinned: "I'll make sure she avoids the whiskey." He held out his hand. "Come on, Laura, we have to go through security; our flight has been called."

"Colin!" David Mornay straightened and, in doing so, gave a

quick grimace of pain. "Thank you again for doing this. I'm sorry that you're going to miss some of the semester."

"No, Uncle Dave; since Kate . . ." he paused, then firmly, "since the accident, I can't concentrate. This'll be a much needed distraction. I have to get away from here."

The two men watched as Colin and Laura put their hand luggage on the moving belt and walked through the partition into the security room where they were hidden from view.

"I'm not sure you shouldn't have waited until after your operation," Rafa murmured as they turned to leave the departure concourse.

"I never told you, did I?" David Mornay patted his pockets as a final check. "After we left Namibia, Kate was still very weak and we spent months recuperating with her parents in South Africa. Jack and Trish Scott were incredibly kind to me. I owe them both a huge debt. Now that Jack has had this heart attack, I'm certain due to the news of Kate's death, I can't deny his wish to see his granddaughter."

"I know, Dave, but your operation shouldn't take that long. I worry about Laura. Damn it, why does everything happen at once?"

"I didn't want her to leave either, but the trip was arranged, and you know what heart attacks are like. The old man could go at any time and I'm forbidden to fly until after the operation. The doc is scared this bloody piece of shrapnel in my neck might migrate further and cut the artery." He rubbed his neck reflectively. "Funny, isn't it? Twenty-eight years later and up pops a little reminder of the battle for Hue."

"You never knew before; felt it, I mean?"

"No. I knew there were the odd small grenade fragments in my back that the medics couldn't get out, but I've never had trouble, apart from the odd twinge, until now. Only when I had those pains after the funeral and you and Nigel made me have a check-up did it show on the X-ray." He scowled at nothing in particular, causing a young man coming through the automatic doors to look away hastily. "I still find it hard to believe that a piece of metal can travel like a mole. Well, if all goes as planned, we should be joining them in two weeks."

"Your operation is scheduled for after the weekend then?"

"Yes. I go in Sunday afternoon and they operate sometime Monday morning, so I should be home early Tuesday." David Mornay looked at his friend. "What about your charter business in Chile? I feel guilty that you've been here for three weeks now and don't mind coming to South Africa with me."

Rafa laughed. "I haven't had a decent break in three years. How long did I spend with you and Kate last year, eh? Two days—all of two days, and then only because I was picking up another aircraft from the brokers in Calgary. No, my friend, this trip to South Africa and Namibia will be a tonic for both of us." He paused outside the building, looking up at the clearing sky with the obsessive stare of a professional airman. "Anyway, Julio Alvarez is very competent. I have no worries on that score. The business will probably run better for me not being around for a few weeks."

David grunted. "I'm not sure that Nigel hasn't set you up to nursemaid me—you mustn't let him convince you—he's a master salesman, if nothing else."

Rafa stopped walking towards the car park, forcing David to slow and finally turn towards him. Rafa's face was grave but his eyes were steady: "I loved her too, Dave. I don't want to grieve on my own, and neither do you. So let's not pretend we can survive this without each other's help."

David Mornay nodded and half-lifted both hands. "I know . . . I know; Sorry, it wasn't meant to . . ." Then firmly, his voice strengthening, " . . . come on, let *me* buy *you* lunch for a change."

The two men resumed their journey towards where the limousine and chauffeur waited.

As he pulled out of the airport parking lot, George Lundquist adjusted the rearview mirror and studied the two men sitting in the luxurious leather back seat of the Lincoln Continental. As personal driver for the last ten years to Nigel Mornay, George knew as much about his boss's older brother, David, as did few outside the family. He knew that David had been the family's black sheep and was just a teenager when he turned his back on the Mornay fortune and his bullying, sadistic father to join the American Marines. He knew that, after returning from Vietnam, David had joined the giant ConAmGeo corporation and, for the next twenty years, had worked on remote mine sites around the globe, rising steadily to a senior position as their chief of construction.

Glancing at David in his mirror, he was saddened to see how tired David looked; the strong face drawn and lined. This was a man who had done much with his life. If anyone had earned the right to a little happiness he had. Kate and David had been exceptionally happy. Now Kate was dead. In the last seven years, George had come to know and respect the quiet man who very rarely could be persuaded to leave his farm in the Fulford Valley of Saltspring Island and visit the city. When Kate and little Laura did manage to persuade David to join them on their occasional forays to Victoria or Vancouver, Nigel insisted that George chauffeur them around. While his wife and daughter plundered the shops in Victoria, David would prevail upon George to join him downtown in the 'Sticky Wicket' pub. The two men would talk of sport while they waited for the women to join them for lunch. From scraps of overheard conversation between Kate and David, George understood that David had refused to be drawn into the day-to-day operations of Mornay Industries, preferring instead to act as the organisation's mining expert when new acquisitions were being negotiated.

Remembering Kate Mornay, George sighed. She had been such a lovely person, twelve years younger than her husband, full of quick laughter and genuine kindnesses. When little Laura was born, George had seen the anticipation and love pour out from the normally reserved David. It was only Kate's commonsense that prevented the child from being very spoilt.

"Where to, Mr. Mornay?" George spoke without turning his head.

"I think the Oak Tree Hotel, George."

George nodded and swung the wheel to leave the Pat Bay Highway for McKenzie Avenue and then through the university grounds down the more scenic route along Beach Drive.

O'Doull waited for Davis to walk through the metal detectors ahead of him. Despite all the assurances given by Rostov, he wanted a cushion between himself and the Swede in case the weapons the Swede carried triggered an alarm. Directly in front of him a young man, holding the hand of a little girl, placed their hand luggage on the conveyor. O'Doull smiled inwardly as a brown teddy bear rolled out of sight under the rubber strips; he wondered how his own daughter was doing with that bitch he had divorced. The Swede was through the detector gate and was busy collecting his hand luggage before O'Doull took a deep breath and placed the hard plastic Samsonite case on the conveyor. He walked towards the detector gate, feeling perspiration trickle down his arms under the casual lightweight jacket, and willed himself to relax. After all, this wasn't the first time he'd had to pass through what was, in a manner of speaking, enemy territory. He saw the Swede swing the lightweight backpack over one shoulder and grasp the duty free parcel in his other hand.

Two days before, in a rented downtown Vancouver Eastside hotel room, O'Doull had met the Swede for the first time and realised that, as with Rostov, he was in the company of a very dangerous man. They had exchanged the codewords of their trade and retired to O'Doull's room where the Swede briefed O'Doull on the minor changes to the plan outlined by Rostov three weeks before. O'Doull suspected that his partner was neither a Swede nor was Davis his real name, but in their world that was normal. Something about Davis stirred his memory, and he recalled a meeting he'd attended in New York four years before, a meeting between top IRA politicals and their American backers in which the name of a contract killer called 'The Swede' had surfaced. Watching Davis stride confidently down the corridor, he wondered if this was the same man. Shrugging, he collected his case and followed the flow to the waiting-room.

O'Doull was a leftover from the glory days of the IRA. As a boy runner for the provisionals, he'd graduated to surveillance duties and finally the bomb squads that took the war directly to the British troops trying to hold the line between Protestant and Catholic extremists. A failed ambush left him the only survivor. Savagely pursued by a wasps' nest of SAS, he had fled to Europe and down the escape pipeline to Madrid where he assumed a new identity and waited for instructions that never came. While O'Doull sat in uncomfortable exile, the British Government's new peace initiative wound down the bitter, unwinnable war in Ireland, and both sides accepted an uneasy peace. Forgotten and unable to return home until advised that it was safe to, O'Doull began to put out feelers of his own. A chance meeting with an old Basque ally led him to an organisation that was recruiting good men for a yet-unspecified operation. Sitting alone one evening in Café La Paloma, drinking the miserable Spanish excuse for beer, he felt the hairs on his neck prickle and knew he was being watched. All his old dread of the SAS surfaced. Slowly downing the tepid brew, he planned his escape carefully. With studied nonchalance he went to the bar and ordered another beer and, dropping enough coins on the counter, asked the barman for directions to the men's washroom. But, instead of going to the men's room, he kept on down the dim passage before cutting through a side door into an empty office and out the open window into a side alley. The following day his Basque contact knocked on his door and, when identified and inside, grinned broadly.

"By God, Brendan, you really impressed the 'White Fire' boys last night." He laughed throatily. "Now you see him, now you don't . . . Ha! They want to meet. Can you be at the Trocadero tonight at eight?"

"White Fire?" O'Doull leaned back on the unmade bed. "What the hell's White Fire?"

"The program I told you about." He tossed a small packet of US dollar bills onto the bed. "Five hundred dollars even if you don't go, and there's another five hundred if you do." He squinted into the wall mirror, setting the beret more rakishly on his head. "These boys are professionals. They've been watching you, and last night made sure you knew . . . just to see how you would react. Actually, it's quite a compliment they've given you, non?"

And so he met Kassim and Rostov and was told of Davis. Over the next three days of intense discussions, the plan unfolded. Now he sauntered down the corridor with other passengers bound for Flight 809.

Chapter 3

Ottawa - Parliament buildings

Dar Yassin spun the gold pen between his fingers. "No," he said angrily, "there must be reparations! For years we have suffered under Israeli exploitation." He glanced at Ali Khufra to judge his reaction, but the commander of all Hamas field units and vice-chairman of the movement did not glance up from the pad on which he was doodling.

Yassin continued, raising his voice and ignoring Professor Watson, the tame PLO apologist, and Abu Hakim, the deputy chairman of the PLO. "We will continue the struggle no matter what secret deals the Zionists make with lackeys." This a direct reference to Egypt and now possibly Syria. "We expect full reparations and significantly more land than has been offered." He stopped, and his eyes flicked around the small room. He watched carefully for any sign or expression on the Russian's face but, like Khufra, UN Delegate Viktor Kuchinsky stared down at the polished table.

The Sudanese UN delegate asked quietly, "And what of those Palestinians who have agreed to the Israeli's terms; are you prepared to negotiate with them?"

"No, but they must be re-educated . . ."

Burt Cunningham, the Canadian coordinator, sat quietly in his chair, his head, with its thatch of snow white hair, tilted down, his eyes half closed as if asleep. He had not missed one word. Now, as the next PLO delegate rose to speak, Dar Yassin concluded his address to the small group gathered in the main conference room of the Parliament Buildings. Cunningham picked out the significant items which he thought wryly were no more than an overstatement of previously held views. He wondered where Mike Monroe had disappeared to so suddenly; a UN representative, especially, should wait until the meeting officially ended.

In the hallway, Mike Monroe, Canada's United Nations

representative, spoke urgently into the telephone: "Les, it's too good a chance to pass up. Both groups have expressed the desire to see more of Canada than conference rooms in Ottawa." His face registered exasperation as he waited for the other party to finish. "I know it's nothing to do with Victoria but, for heaven's sake, man, they're world news at the moment. Just think of the publicity and the tourist potential."

Something was said. Monroe chuckled and continued in a more conciliatory tone. "Les, it's not for my sake. Of course I'd like any help I can get in the next election, but, come now, the idea has merit, don't you think?" This time the answer must have pleased Monroe who now smiled broadly. "You won't regret this, Les. After all, the feds will fund the travel and security costs. All the city council has to do is invite the group with the maximum amount of publicity and provide accommodation for a couple of nights."

In Victoria, Mayor Les Patterson thought quickly. "How long will they stay?"

"Only three days, Les. Just two nights. Surely the council can afford the accommodation."

"Yes, yes, it can come out of the tourist budget. But explain to me again how having this delegation will benefit us. Remember, I still have to get council on side."

Monroe had often expressed the sentiment that politics was a game for patient men and so restrained himself. "OK, Les. The groups now in Ottawa consist of three UN observers, of which I am one, as you know, and two groups of Palestinians, the PLO and Hamas. The federal government invited them to hold their meetings in Canada which is considered neutral territory by both groups, especially since our prime minister met with Yasser Arafat. So far, the meetings have been going well but there are still sticking points, and I feel that a bit of a break in Victoria—a working vacation so to speak—might be the answer."

"I still don't see . . ."

"Wait a second, Les! As you know, the latest American and European initiatives are going nowhere. If Canada can show that it's the country that finally helps to crack this issue, think of the advantages to us in terms of foreign trade, especially with the Middle East." He paused for a second. "The meetings in Ottawa are scheduled to end tomorrow and, to be honest, they've not been as successful as we'd hoped. There are dozens of correspondents covering this conference. If Victoria invites all the delegates to end their stay in Canada with a brief holiday there, think of the coverage, of the impression it would give." He waited. The silence lengthened. "Les?"

"OK, Mike. I'll call a meeting of the council tonight and put it to them, but I can't promise the outcome."

"Thanks, Les. I know you won't regret this. Please give Gwen my regards; I'll treat you both to a meal when this is all over."

Michael James Monroe, Canada's United Nations representative was, at 42, the youngest ever. A sociologist and former university lecturer, he had come to prominence following the Rock Point Prison scandal when his masterly analysis of the prison system had initiated major reforms. His report had won praise from law makers and enforcement agencies but his more doctrinaire associates had labelled him right-wing and fascist. Monroe had felt the pulse of popular opinion and, with political ambitions of his own, he had needed a vessel to carry his aspirations. The scandal had broken at just the right time and he had recommended a much harder line. He replaced the receiver and walked back into the conference room, unaware that he was smiling broadly, and was startled when Ali Al-Azhar, the Sudanese UN observer, asked softly,

"Good news, Dr. Monroe?"

"Oh .., Ali, I didn't notice you . . . Yes, it might be, but I have to wait until tomorrow to be sure."

"It is not, I take it, connected with our discussions here," Al-Azhar indicated the long table at which a dozen men sat in loud conversation. "No one is betting on a joint communiqué tomorrow; the best we can hope for is a declaration of intent." His thin aquiline face broke into a smile. "Still, who knows?

These days it is wiser to be a pessimist."

Monroe smiled back. He liked the swarthy Sudanese and often wondered about him. Al-Azhar talked fiery rhetoric in public, castigating the Great Powers for their lack of sensitivity to the problems of the Middle East. In private, however, he admitted to the conviction that many problems in the Middle East were self-induced and that self-serving power structures had, for too long, acted as a brake on positive development. It was said he was related to the Sudanese president, but Ali had laughed when the subject had been raised: "Good Lord, no; not at all. Al-Azhar is a fairly common name. Still, it would have been good for my career had it been so." Rumour also maintained that he had served as head of the secret police until some fall from grace had sent him to the UN as Sudan's representative. None of this was certain, and Ali himself never discussed his background, deflecting questions with subtle wit and charm. Viktor Kuchinsky, the third member of the UN observer group, sat some distance away, talking quietly to Ali Khufra. The Hamas commander was nodding at something Kuchinsky was describing, the Russian's hand making designs in the air as he emphasised the point he was making. Physically, Kuchinsky was as different from the stereotypical Russian as it was possible to be. Tall, urbane and cultured, a distinguished 55-year-old, he was reputed to be a hardliner who would welcome a return to the iron control of the former communist regime. Speaking with Kuchinsky, one was often totally disarmed by his apparent candour and delightful humour that hid, Monroe felt, a cold and ruthless mind. Khufra was also ruthless, cold and impassive, but, where Kuchinsky would use a stiletto, Khufra would use a club. Khufra's arrogance during the past week had caused friction between the two groups, and his remark about Professor Peter Watson, the only non-Arab among the delegates, being the 'Token White' had not improved the situation. Watson had long espoused the Arab cause, and his rabid, one-sided stand had alienated all but the most left-wing among his Canadian colleagues. His articles and scholarly papers, while often brilliantly composed, verged on being anti-Semitic; yet to listen to the man was to marvel at the apparent sincerity of his views.

"Gentlemen, please." This from Burt Cunningham, the Canadian coordinator of the meeting. "It's been a long day . . . can we agree to adjourn and resume at 10 a.m. tomorrow in this room?" A rumble of agreement came from the delegates, but Monroe noted that Khufra and Kuchinsky had not even given notice they had heard. He turned to Al-Azhar with a smile and said jokingly, "Perhaps our friends over there have solved the problem."

Kuchinsky must have heard for he lifted his head and looked coldly at Monroe. Monroe raised his hand as if to greet the Russian, then dropped it, feeling mildly embarrassed. Kuchinsky suddenly smiled and his eyes came alive. "Hello, Mike. No, we haven't solved the problem, but we're working on it." Khufra said nothing, his face impassive. The Canadian felt a ripple of anger. He had tried often to draw the Hamas man into social dialogue, but without success. He looked back to Kuchinsky.

"Well, one more day of deliberations does not give us much time to get an agreement."

Kuchinsky lifted his hands in mock supplication. "Who knows what tomorrow will bring, doctor." He smiled broadly as he rose to his feet. "Sleep well, gentlemen; I'm for an early night."

Monroe was surprised at the sudden look of concern that crossed Khufra's face at Kuchinsky's remark about the morning. Shrugging, he dismissed the incident. Later, much later, he would remember it.

The room was emptying fast as Al-Azhar and Monroe turned to leave. "Care for a drink, Ali? I have a very nice malt in my suite."

The Sudanese hesitated fractionally, then nodded and fell into step beside Monroe. "Tell me, Mike, are you married?"

Monroe took a deep breath. "Yes, my wife lives in Vancouver on the West Coast. Why do you ask?"

"No reason . . . I just wondered, when you left the room

earlier, if you were phoning home since you returned so obviously pleased." He raised a hand, shaking his head. "You must forgive me. I do not intend to pry, but I sometimes fancy myself as an amateur Sherlock Holmes. It is inexcusable bad manners."

Monroe smiled, relieved that the sad saga of his marriage would not surface. "Nothing to forgive, Ali. It's a habit we're all prone to, I suspect. Actually, I was trying to arrange a visit to Victoria. Perhaps a change of venue will set a more positive tone to these meetings." He nodded to a colleague passing in the corridor. "Please treat this as confidential. I am hoping to get confirmation early tomorrow."

"I see. Victoria is on Vancouver Island?"

"You have been there?"

"No, never, but a cousin of my sister-in-law lives there. I have always wanted to visit."

"Well, the official invitation should arrive tomorrow."

"Excellent, excellent! Let us hope all goes as wished . . . no, planned . . . 'planned' is the correct word, is it not? My English is not as perfect as I would like."

"Your English is nearly perfect, my friend. Tell me, are you married?"

"Ha . . . who would have me, an old and desiccated diplomat? I recall a story of a man who walked through a forest looking to cut a fine walking-stick. Every likely one he saw he passed by, as a better one might be just ahead. Soon he was out of the wood and still he had no suitable stick. So it is with me. I'm out of the wood, Michael."

Monroe chuckled and, changing the subject, asked, "What's the chance of getting a joint agreement if we extend the talks . . . ?"

The two men, one tall, fair and well-built, the other short, swarthy and slight, made a study in contrast as they walked down the passage talking quietly.

Chapter 4

Day 1: 2100 hrs, local.

Empress Hotel - Victoria

David surfaced, the gunfire fading as the dream died. Kate had been running from the Viet Cong, while Major Hovass led a group of marines through a bamboo thicket topped by a column of coloured smoke. Three small children were dancing on the cloud and laughing at the antics of the humans below.

The phone rang again. David shook his head; the dream already gone. "Yes?"

"David. Is that you, David?"

"Scottie . . . ?" Puzzled, David sat up. Kate's father never telephoned. What the hell was going on? He swung his legs clear of the bed and ran stiffened fingers through his hair. "What's up, Scottie? Colin and Laura aren't with you already, are they?"

"No . . . that's . . . David, I have some bad news. Apparently the plane they were on has been hijacked and . . ."

"Hijacked? . . . hijacked! . . . who . . . ? My God, Scottie . . . What are you saying? Who the hell would hijack their plane? . . . are you sure?"

The older man could hear the stunned disbelief in his son-in-law's voice. "David, I'm sorry, but we've just heard about it from our early morning news. I called the airline immediately and they confirmed the hijacking. There is very little hard news at the moment, and I'm sure that you'll get all the latest at your end more quickly than we will here."

"Jesus, Scottie, . . . who the hell are they after . . . why this plane?" David stared at the bedroom wall. A framed print of Rufino Tamayo's 'Figure Radiant with Joy,' which Rafa had given him on the birth of Laura six years ago, stood resting against the wall. He had retrieved the painting earlier the previous afternoon from Art Bank Framing in Bastion Square. Kate had decided on a new frame; it was one of the last items she had handled before her death. His stomach felt hollow, and a faint nausea rose in his throat.

"I don't know . . . No one does at the moment . . . Look, are you all right? I'm sure Laura will be all right with Colin."

"Damn it, Scottie, I should have waited! Rafa wanted me to. . ." Suddenly remembering, "Judas Priest, Scottie, I'm sorry . . . I should be asking you how your heart is holding up. How are you feeling?"

"I'm a lot tougher than these bloody quacks give me credit for. Now listen to me, David; I want you and Rafa to keep me up to date with all the latest news. Nigel will have access to sources, and I want to be kept informed. Don't you worry about Trish and me; we'll hold our end up."

David smiled sadly to himself. His father-in-law was as tough as leather, but years of hard work as a farmer in Kenya and the expropriation of his beloved farm had left scars. Now, though suffering from the aftermath of a heart attack, he was trying to cheer David up—a heart attack that David believed had been brought on by the news of his daughter's death. "Of course! Scottie, I'm going to call Nigel right now and get him to start using his influence. Look, don't phone the hotel again. I'm going to be in and out, so phone Nigel's private number. Do you have a pen handy? OK, here it is. . . ." David read off the digits slowly and repeated the number twice. "I'll have someone from the office man that phone round the clock." He rubbed his face, his mind going into high gear as the full import of what had happened sank in. "Scottie, I'll call you back within the next two hours. Give Trish a hug from me and tell her that we'll get them back. That I promise." He placed the phone back in its cradle and immediately dialled another number. Holding the phone tensely, he waited, then spoke quickly. "Rafa, Laura and Colin's plane has been hijacked . . . I'll explain later . . . Meet me in the lobby as soon as you can." Pushing the cut-off button, he dialled again. "Nigel, it's David. Scottie has just phoned to tell me that Laura and Colin's plane has been hijacked . . . wait,

wait . . . I don't know any more than what I've told you. Rafa
and I are on our way to your house. Can you rev up your people
to start getting more information? . . . No, don't wait for us; get
started right away . . . yes, I'll be there in 15 minutes."

David started stripping his pyjamas off and rummaging for
clothes in the wall-length closet. Choosing a light blue denim
shirt and faded jeans, he pulled wool socks over his feet which
he pushed into soft moccasin loafers. Scooping up his wallet
and credit card holder, he pocketed his car keys, locked the door
behind him, and dropped the hotel key into his pocket.

Chapter 5

Day 2:   0400 hrs.

Over the Atlantic

Colin stared at the three men patrolling the aisles. It was still hard to believe the events of the last few hours. The United Airlines flight from Vancouver to Kennedy Airport in New York had been smooth and on time. Sitting with Laura in business class, they'd been pampered and fussed over by the cabin crew. The stewardess had been captivated by the quiet, grave-faced little girl and her big cousin. Laura had dozed on and off during the seven-hour flight and the two-hour wait in New York. After exiting the transit lounge and transferring to South African Airways, she had suddenly perked up as the 747 lifted into the night sky over JFK.

"Colin." She tugged at his sleeve. "Grandma and Batchi will be waiting at the next stop?"

Colin put his magazine aside. "Yes, they'll be there to pick us up and take us to Batchi's farm." For some reason, when she was two years old, on one of her semi-annual visits, she had called her Grandfather 'Batchi' and the name had stuck. It had always been an enjoyable time for David, Kate and Laura on the five-acre hobby farm that Kate's father had turned into a showcase 15 years earlier. Jack Scott and his wife had left Kenya when their 1,000 acre highland farm had been expropriated and moved to South Africa with their daughter, Kate. With dogged perseverance, Jack had slowly turned the five acres of semi-scrub highveld into a nursery of beautiful flowering trees, shrubs and row-on-row of flowers for the cut-flower market in Johannesburg.

Kate had grown into a lovely woman, taken a degree in chemistry, and then married the business major who'd pursued her at university. Kate's marriage to Jack Richardson had disintegrated while they were both working at the same mine as

David Mornay. Kate had met David by accident, then, through a series of events that led to David's hospitalisation after a mine accident, she'd fallen deeply in love with the construction chief. Jack Scott had never taken to his first son-in-law whom he considered far too ambitious and self-centred. Scottie had always felt that Kate had made a mistake, and when Kate's marriage finally dissolved she had brought David to her parents' home to recuperate after his accident. Her father had taken to the quiet construction boss the instant they met. The two men were similar: doers rather than talkers, both had been scarred by life and this had hardened and toughened them. Both were devoted to Kate and, when Laura had been born, they had been beside themselves with excitement and pride.

Once a year, from the time Laura could travel, David and Kate had flown to South Africa to share their daughter with her grandparents. Now the lovely Kate was dead, and the impact on the two men who loved her most was savage. Jack Scott suffered a mild heart attack and was warned to severely restrict his activities. To a casual observer, David appeared unchanged. Never a person to share his emotions, he seemed a little quieter and perhaps more reserved than usual, but nothing on the surface showed the damage occurring inside. After the funeral, Rafa, worried about David, extended his stay. Then a medical check-up revealed shrapnel in David's neck close to the carotid artery, and Rafa insisted on remaining until the operation to remove the dangerous metal was over.

Realising that the one thing that would help Scottie and Trish overcome the loss of their daughter was to have their grandchild visit, David had been on the verge of travelling with Laura to see them when the medical check revealed the shrapnel in his neck. During the battle for Hue in Vietnam, David had been badly wounded by an exploding grenade. Some shrapnel had evaded the surgeons' attempts at extraction,—now a piece no bigger than a fingernail was threatening his life.

All of these thoughts passed through Colin's mind while he marvelled at the synchronised events that had placed Laura and himself on a hijacked jumbo. The hijackers had revealed themselves an hour after take off. How they could have brought weapons on board was a mystery to Colin until he recognised a hijacker from their departure lounge in Vancouver and, with a sinking feeling, remembered how cursory the security checks had been at that early hour. The main group must have boarded in New York and received their weapons from the men who had boarded in Vancouver. As there was no security check in New York's JFK Airport for transit passengers, it would have been a simple matter for the Slavic-looking man to bring the weapons in hand luggage through lax security at Vancouver and, once aboard the SAA jumbo, distribute them to accomplices.

Colin looked back at Laura who seemed totally uninterested in the drama unfolding around them. When the hijackers had stood up in various parts of the aircraft to announce the takeover, most of the passengers were stunned. Who on God's earth would hijack a South African jumbo? Apartheid was dead, a black president ruled the country and, apart from minor tribal conflicts, there was no obvious reason for South Africa to be targeted. The hijackers had been calm, cold and very professional, only one member had spoken and he had assured the passengers that they were not the primary targets and, if they obeyed instructions, would be released within a short time. The hijackers' spokesman, a stocky man with pale, almost colourless eyes and a slight accent that Colin guessed was Scandinavian, moved round the cabin slowly. His eyes flicked over the passengers with the calm detachment a snake gives to the frog before it strikes. Colin saw him point to an older man sitting across the aisle and motion two hijackers to lift him to his feet. Surprisingly the man showed little fear as he was hauled roughly out of business class and up the stairs to the upper deck. The same was not true of the next six people selected. They were plainly terrified, and one woman became hysterical, weeping and struggling until a hijacker slapped her face with enough force to knock her semiconscious. They were herded up the staircase and, moments later, angry voices and the sound of a blow carried clearly to where Colin sat his arm protectively round Laura. As the aircraft droned steadily on through the night sky, Laura began to feel sleepy and, stretching out, fell asleep with her head on Colin's lap. An hour later Colin put down his magazine and was suddenly aware of being watched by a dark-haired woman across the aisle.

"Your daughter seems to be an unusually well-balanced child. How old is she?"

"She's my cousin, not my daughter, and Laura is six years old." Colin found himself fascinated by the woman's voice which had a slightly husky timbre. "I'm sure I've seen you before, somewhere else." Then, seeing the woman smile: "No, no, I mean it! I'm not trying out the old line. I'm sure I recognise you."

"Quite possibly. I'm a foreign correspondent for CNN." She held out her hand across the aisle. "My name is Christine, and yours . . ." She waited.

"Colin Mornay." Colin took the cool dry hand. "Are you on your way to an assignment now?"

Christine laughed dryly, "Compared with what's happening now, nothing quite so exciting, I'm supposed to cover the state visit by the Russian vice-president to South Africa. From past experience they tend to be rather boring affairs." She pointed to Laura. "You're doing a good job of keeping her insulated from the earlier unpleasantness."

Colin remembered where he had seen Christine before. "You were in Bosnia,—weren't you?"

"Yes, for quite a while." Christine brushed a strand of dark glossy hair back from her forehead. She was not beautiful, Colin thought, but had a strong, handsome face and direct dark eyes.

"Have you ever . . ?" he inclined his head in the direction of the hijackers strolling towards them.

"Been hijacked? No, fortunately never, but I've been around a couple from the outside. I still can't figure out what this is all about."

"You can't?—I was just about to ask you what the motive might be—being as you're a foreign correspondent and in touch with this sort of thing." Colin stopped talking as the two hijackers approached and, when they were safely passed, whispered, "Why South Africa? These men are Arab. I didn't think the new government in South Africa had enemies."

"No, nothing makes sense. And their leader, the European fellow who spoke earlier, said that the passengers were not their primary concern. I'm curious why they took some passengers upstairs: All I can think of is that this aircraft is carrying something of value, perhaps in the cargo hold."

"Do you think they will fly us to somewhere in the Middle East?"

"It seems likely, although I would suspect we are going to have to refuel somewhere."

A sudden thought crossed Colin's mind. "And they might bargain for fuel by freeing all the women at that stop. Isn't that a tactic?" He felt suddenly clammy. Laura was in his care. Good God, what should he do? "Look, Christine, can I ask a big favour. If that happens will you take care of Laura? Here," he rummaged in the case at his feet, "here is my home address and phone number." He looked up and down the aisle to make sure no hijackers were in the vicinity before reaching across to hand the card to Christine. "Call and tell them Laura's safe. They'll see you're compensated for any expenses." He lowered his voice to a whisper, making sure that Laura had not stirred, her little chest rising and falling rythmically. "Laura's mother, Kate . . ." he stopped, took a deep breath, then continued, "was killed in a car accident three weeks ago, and her father, my uncle, will be frantic." Quickly he filled the correspondent in on the reasons for his journey with Laura and David's reason for not travelling with them.

Christine nodded gravely. "Of course I will. But you mustn't worry, Colin: they may let everyone off at the next stop. Still, you're wise to think ahead." She removed a card from her purse and, with a silver-ballpoint pen, wrote a number on the back. "You've given me the same idea. Should they decide to keep the women, here is my mother's phone number. If you'd call her it would be a great comfort."

"Keep the women?" Colin was aghast. "Like hell! I won't let them take Laura, . . . do you think they will?"Colin's voice had risen, so Christine wagged a finger warningly across her lips.

"Probably not children, but, as I said before, don't imagine things that may not happen." She smiled reassuringly. "Let's wait and see, shall we. After all there's nothing we can do until they tell us what this is all about." She settled herself more comfortably in the seat. "Tell me about yourself, what do you do . . .?"

The big jet thundered through the night as Colin and Christine whispered across the aisle and Laura slept.

Chapter 6.

Day 2:   0530 hrs.

Rockland Heights - Victoria

David, Rafa and Nigel sat around the polished table in Nigel's study. The room was large, originally a sitting room that after extensive remodelling, could now hold a huge desk and a boardroom table with chairs for ten people. One wall was covered in teak shelving that reached from floor to ceiling. Row upon row of books, most of them rare and all of them expensive, filled the shelves. On the opposite wall, the latest in computer and communications equipment sat discreetly behind cabinet doors that did not completely hide the fact that this was an alternate nerve centre of the huge Mornay conglomerate. A third wall, entirely of glass, looked out on acres of manicured lawn and garden, now turning pink in the early dawn.

Scattered on the table were computer printouts from news sources around the world. A continuous feed printer chattered quietly in the background as its program searched for key words that would identify news of the hijacked plane. At the far end of the table, two senior analysts, dragged from their beds by a peremptory phone call from Nigel Mornay, were pouring over every scrap of information that was piling up on the table before them.

"Well, what have you got?" Nigel growled down the table.

Bayliss, the older of the two analysts, looked up and shook his head. "Nothing that makes any kind of sense. Jim and I are running the TRIDENT program; perhaps that will help. What we have so far is a big fat zero."

"Dammit, man—I pay you two handsome salaries to be on top of information—I don't expect 'a big fat zero,' to quote you." Nigel's frustration was obvious and uncharacteristic.

"Easy, Nigel," David laid a large hand on Nigel's arm. "If there is nothing concrete yet, then that's not Geoff's fault. Geoff, you said something about a TRIDENT program—what's that?"

Throwing a grateful glance at David, Bayliss explained. "You are computer proficient, Mr. Mornay?"

David shook his head. "Not really—not to any level that would impress you, I'm sure."

"It's one of the latest of a series of software programs that were developed in the 70's and continuously upgraded by the CIA to scan all types of radio transmissions. As technology improved, additional features were added, and one of those is the ability to combine discrete items of random information that have a similar fingerprint into what could be best called an intelligent guess. If I can use an example, imagine you are in a crowded room. You overhear conversations from every direction and think, from one fragment of what you are hearing, that a crime is being plotted, but you can't be certain. You strain to hear something else that will confirm or put to rest your now-active imagination. What's happening is that your brain is filtering out all the other extraneous conversations and trying to make a match with the voice or timbre or inflection of the original sentence fragment. Of course, when your hearing relays to your brain the match you're searching for, you realise with relief that the conversation referred to the death of someone's cat. This program goes many levels higher than the simple explanation I've given you. We use it to track and stay on top of technical developments in the mining world."

"How long before you have anything . . . anything at all?" David stared intently at Bayliss. His face was calm, but his eyes flickered like distant lightning on a dark day.

Bayliss spread his hands. "Mr. Mornay, there are—quite literally—millions of pieces of information available at any given minute worldwide. Even with the facilities of the National Security Agency in Washington—which we don't have—it would take time." He looked directly at David. "Nothing so far matches any scenario that makes sense. The South African government has no serious quarrel with internal or external agencies. The hijackers have not stated their aims. The plane has not been diverted and is maintaining its original track towards South Africa. None of the passengers appears important . . ." He stopped. "Damn . . . of course . . ."

David leaned forward tensely; the others stared at Bayliss with undisguised impatience.

"Come on, Geoff, spit it out, for God's sake!" Nigel snapped at Bayliss.

Bayliss ran his hand through thinning hair. "One of the first things Jim and I did was to acquire a list of passengers and check the names for anyone significant—a politician, drug lord, businessman who might be a target. We found nothing that fit. All the passengers were your standard mix of tourists, business people, and low-grade embassy staff." He grimaced, shaking his head slowly. "I obviously can't be sure, but it's possible that there's someone on board that the hijackers want. Someone who is travelling under an assumed name. We don't have the facilities to check into the background of every passenger, but it makes sense for a prominent person to travel incognito so as not to attract media attention, on a mid-week, flight on an airline that has never had a hijacking."

"So now what . . .?" Nigel was stopped in mid-question as a distinctive beeping came from the computer in front of the other analyst, Jim Miles. Bayliss turned swiftly and, in two strides, was leaning over Miles' shoulder. "They've diverted . . . they're apparently heading for West Africa. Satscan/AP reports that the captain is asking for clearance to land at Ilha do Sal."

"Ilha what? Where is that? Bring up the map on the screen." Nigel pointed to a cabinet set flush into the wall. Bayliss stepped sideways and slid the cabinet doors apart, revealing a large, 48" flat-screen TV. Punching a series of buttons on a standard keyboard set into a sliding tray below the screen, he brought up a map of the world that brightened into life as he rolled the contrast wheel. Typing in the name *Ilha do Sal* brought up a large scale view of the West African coast, stretching from Mauritania to the Ivory Coast. Peering at the screen closely, Bayliss grunted with satisfaction. "Here it is." He touched the screen with his finger; immediately it changed to reveal a group of islands positioned off the coast of Senegal. "The Cape Verde Islands—Sal is this one . . ." The four men clustered around the screen.

Nigel spoke quickly to Bayliss: "Geoff, what information can you get on this island? Why would anyone want to land there? It's a tiny dot in the middle of nowhere."

Rafa spoke before Bayliss could answer. "Because they have a runway long enough to take a 747." He turned to David. "Remember when sanctions were imposed on South Africa and SAA was banned from flying over Continental Africa: SAA rerouted over Sal which gave them a refuelling stop on the way to Europe." His swarthy face was grim. "It is the perfect spot to hold an aircraft on the ground while you negotiate whatever it is you're after."

Jim Miles spoke from his position at the main computer console. "I have a late-breaking message follow-up. It appears that the airport and surrounding area have been taken over as well. Sal tower is not responding to requests from Interpol, but they are talking to the 747." He turned back to the screen that was scrolling continuous information: "Oh, oh, . . . what's this? The hijackers are asking for a clear satlink channel. They must have some very sophisticated equipment with them."

Stunned, the men stared at each other. David broke the silence. "Whatever is happening, this is big, very big. This is not some bunch of disaffected elements trying to make a point." His face was chalk white and the line of his jaw was set and grim.

Chapter 7

Midday:

Ilha do Sal - Espargos Airfield

Ilha do Sal, the 'Island of Salt,' 83 square miles of sand, its flatness broken by a few saline hills and notable for only two things: its exports of salt to Portugal and the airport of Espargos, capable of accepting the largest passenger aircraft in service.

During the 60's and 70's, South African Airways saw their traditional stopping points on the way to Europe denied them. Nairobi, Khartoum and Cairo were blocked by nationalistic governments who did not want to be accused by the African National Congress of helping the racist government of South Africa. Forced by circumstance, the South Africans first flew from Johannesburg to Salisbury in Rhodesia and then over Portuguese-held Angola, out into the South Atlantic, and up past the western bulge of Africa to Lisbon. It was a brutal test of aircrews and aircraft, for the margins were fine and a stopping point had to be found. Ilha do Sal, lying like a pebble cast into the sea off the coast of Senegal at position Lat. 16 45' North, Long. 23 West, almost halfway between Luanda in Angola and Lisbon in Portugal, was the perfect answer. The airport at Espargos was quickly upgraded to take the largest aircraft then flying, and the terminal was cleaned and upgraded to cope with over three thousand passengers a week. When Angola fell to the Marxist MPLA in 1977, South Africa swung from using Luanda to Windhoek in South West Africa, but Ilha do Sal remained a vital link in their system.

Now the giant 747 in the orange, blue and white livery of South African Airways sat on the apron in the sparkling sunshine. The airport, seen by most travellers only at night, now sported armed men on the roof and others lounging in the shade of the verandah. The seizure was total: the airport, aircraft, and all ground facilities were in the hands of the hijackers and their accomplices. On a tiny island that a large force could approach only by sea, and then with difficulty, the hijackers were in total command.

The passengers sat mutely aboard: some trying to sleep, others reading, and still others staring into space. It was hot and would have been much worse but for the air-conditioning plant that whined away softly. On the flight deck, Captain Johannes Strydom waited for the next set of instructions. A longtime veteran of South African Airways and one of the few remaining who remembered landing at Ilha do Sal in the 70's, he still could not fully believe that this was happening to his aircraft. The rest of the flight-deck crew had been unceremoniously ejected from the flight deck and now sat under guard in the first-class cabin. All captains fear a hijacking and are trained repeatedly on methods to use in handling the situation but, he thought sourly, it always happens to the other guy. All he could do now was wait. The Irishman didn't worry him. He smiled a lot, made jokes, and even though his eyes never softened, he seemed to be totally relaxed. The Arab who stood in the doorway was another matter. This man the captain measured as a true psychopath. He shivered slightly, hoping that the Irishman or whoever was in charge could keep control of all the men under his command.

The man looking through the huge window into the Washington evening did not turn when the door opened behind him.

"How did they know?" His voice had the husky quality that comes from too many cigarettes over too long a period. The man who had just entered did not reply immediately. He closed the door with a soft click, and opening the folder stamped EYES ONLY—CODE ONE, walked towards the man at the window. "We're still not sure that he's the primary target. Here look at this."

"For God's sake, Jack, it's more than just coincidence." Edward Mason still did not turn from the window to face his deputy chief of operations. "Don't try to tell me that we picked the one airline that was due for a hijack—statistical averages or something."

"No, sir." Jack Dehenny sighed. He had worked with his boss for more than 25 years and they made a good team. He knew what was going through Mason's mind, and the unthinkable was now a very real possibility. "But it is more than passing strange that Eli Natan is on board that aircraft. Our resident at JFK recognised him, but didn't log the sighting until the end of his shift." Dehenny raised his hand, as if to ward off a blow as Mason spun around. "I know, I know! But hell, Ed, he naturally assumed that we were aware that MOSSAD'S top agent was outbound. After all, Eli was in here talking to me only last week."

Edward Mason stood absolutely still. Plastic surgery gave his face a blankness that was hard to penetrate; only his eyes expressed emotion, and Dehenny saw a spark of hope flare in their dark depths. "What's Tel Aviv saying?"

"They apologise for the oversight in not advising us but, as you know, this trip has been on the card for months. Eli has wanted to take a trip to South Africa for a long time; his father was born there. Eli went incognito for all the usual reasons."

"A mole inside their operation?"

"That's the most viable working hypothesis now. Apparently Eli left at very short notice and his cover as a Lebanese-American businessman is watertight."

"You realise we may be building the wrong construct. Mossad may not be the target. We could be the target, and Eli being on this particular plane is nothing but an incredible coincidence."

Jack Dehenny sighed. "Yes, and we could have the mole." There, it had finally been said; the one thing they both dreaded. "Look, Ed, we've kept the whole operation on a strict need-to-know basis. All the people involved have top clearance."

"Oh yes, and what about that suave prick in the president's office?"

"He only knew the outline, not the details. There's no way he could've, . . . assuming he is the leak, marked CANCEL . . .

absolutely no way."

"Jack, we have to assume that this hijacking is tied in some way with CANCEL. I feel it in my bones. Get the brains trust going over all the information, but isolate them until further notice."

"Yes, I thought of that as well. I'll set it up right away."

"Jack, too much is at stake here. I want full checks run and, if necessary, rerun on everyone who is involved with CANCEL'S mission."

Dehenny shook his head. "No, Ed, let's wait. If we start stirring things up at this end, it might just flag the hijackers, if Eli Natan is their target, to look closer at the other passengers."

Mason turned back to the window. The silence deepened before the two men. When Mason spoke it was barely above a whisper. "You're right, of course . . . but call the White House; we'll have to brief the President."

"Do you want me along?"

"Yes. It's your operation. You should be there."

Midday: **Espargos - Ilha do Sal**

The door to the cockpit opened, and a middle-aged man in faded denims entered. His presence dominated the small cockpit. He pointed to the door. "Go and have some coffee, Kassim. I need to have the captain talk to the world."

The Arab smiled mirthlessly; "I wish to listen—this is a historic moment." The man in denim turned, and Strydom noted that his eyes were almost colourless. Denim paused to stare at the one called Kassim.

"Very well—ask O'Doull to come forward as well." He jerked his head, dismissing the Arab.

"My name is Davis, captain. I have opened a Satlink channel and patched it through to the tower. Anything you say to the tower is relayed to wherever we wish. Do you understand? . . .

Good. Also understand that, by using the tower as a relay, we can delay any heroic attempt to pass restricted information." His craggy face broke into a smile. "Don't worry, captain; no one is going to get hurt." He handed Strydom a typewritten sheet. "Read that out, captain: just as if you were asking for clearance. Speak slowly and clearly."

Strydom took the paper, cleared his throat, and began reading. "This is the 24th November group. We hold the aircraft and passengers, and require the immediate release of all Hamas members in Israeli jails. There will be no further communications until this instruction has been carried out." Strydom cleared his throat and continued with the final paragraph. "Starting at 2400 hours local time, that is, 17 hours from now—we will begin executing one passenger every 15 minutes unless we have received confirmation that our people have been released." Strydom stopped, shaking the paper at the pale-eyed man: "Good God, man, you've just told me that no one is going to get hurt —this would be murder."

The craggy face showed no emotion. "Captain, I sincerely hope that the Israelis obey the instructions, then no one will get hurt, but, just so they believe we are serious - look outside."

Unwillingly, Strydom turned to where the man was indicating. Out on the hardstand, 30 feet from the cockpit, two men in camouflage uniforms held a stewardess by her arms. Strydom recognised her; she was the new girl just graduated from domestic flights to the long-haul routes. She had brought him coffee only a few hours before. Suddenly understanding and horrified, he turned back to the pale-eyed man: "Dear God, no . . . please, she's just a child," he pleaded. Kassim gripped his hair and wrenched his face back to the tableau outside. The girl was forced to her knees, and a third man, dressed like the others stepped up behind the terrified stewardess and on a signal from the cockpit, raised his pistol and shot the girl through the head.

"No! . . . you bastards . . .!" Strydom was struggling to his feet when a pistol slammed against his head, stunning him and bringing blood from a cut over his eyes.

"Calm yourself, captain. I will have the rest of the cabin crew shot right now if you don't settle down." The pale-eyed man handed Strydom a cloth from a pocket in the seat back. "Hold that over your forehead." Watching the captain dab at his head with an unsteady hand, the Arab called Kassim giggled: a high-pitched, unnerving sound.

Strydom felt nausea rising and fought to control it. He felt dizzy, and his anger faded as fear gripped his mind. These men were killers, psychopaths; they would have no more feeling about killing all the cabin crew than they would have about swatting a fly.

"Good, I see we have your full attention, captain. Now, call the tower and tell them what has just happened." Pale-eyes tapped the headset lightly. "Now, please!"

Strydom keyed the microphone. Still feeling sick, he gave a flat monotonous account of the death of the stewardess.

"Excellent, captain! I sincerely hope your description does the trick. I would be very unhappy to have to kill all the passengers." He rose to leave the cockpit. "O'Doull, you take the co-pilot's seat and keep our captain company. Come with me, Kassim." The two men left the cockpit.

Washington: 11am

The president shook hands with the two men from the CIA. He gestured towards a squat man in military uniform and another two standing in the shadows outside the pools of light cast by the floor lamps . "You both know General Denning, Jake Carroll, and Max, so let's start with a review of what we have."

The five men moved to chairs facing the president, and Edward Mason looked at Jack Dehenny. "Jack, you do the honours."

"Mr. President, what we have is the hijacking of a South African airliner by an element of Hamas determined to undermine the peace accord between Israel and the PLO. On this aircraft is a top Mossad agent who was on a private visit to

South Africa. As you know, we also have our own agent en-route to execute the CANCEL contract." He paused, but no one spoke. "We believe that the Israeli network has been compromised and that the hijackers had advance information on the Mossad agent's trip. At this time there is no indication that the CANCEL contract has been compromised."

The president exploded: "And where does that leave us— how long is the window?"

"Another three days, sir." Dehenny felt his stomach contract. He had heard of those famous rages, and the president's sheer size was intimidating.

"Mr. Director," the president's voice was icy as he turned to look at Ed Mason, "I want to know how you managed to send CANCEL on the same aircraft as a known Israeli agent. Who is responsible?"

Ed Mason had served in various positions under two presidents and he would outlast this one. Grimacing, he looked up from hands that lay folded in his lap. "It was a fluke, one of those combinations that cannot be predicted. Normally the Israelis advise us ahead of any proposed movements in and out of the US. Two weeks ago, for Eli Natan, they did; but that trip was cancelled at the last minute. Somehow, whoever handles their liaison assumed that the rescheduled departure had been advised. I'm afraid everyone thought everyone else had done the work." He looked straight at the president. "Obviously, had we known, we would've made alternate arrangements."

The president let his breath out in a rush. "Mr. Director, as you are well aware, what we have riding on CANCEL is of critical importance to the United States and, I believe, the world. We cannot under any circumstances let this operation be compromised." He glared at Ed Mason, "That is why I have asked the chairman of the JCS and the national security advisor to be present." He turned to General Denning. "General, you were advised as soon as the hijacking occurred. Can you outline what contingency planning is underway."

The general opened a flat file on his lap. For such a powerfully built man, his voice was thin and high, but no one in the room had illusions about the brain that lay behind it. "A team of Navy Seals and Rangers are airborne to Portugal and units of the Mediterranean fleet are making for the area, but we have no vessels closer than three days' sailing. Airborne units normally stationed in West Germany are on a mountain exercise in Norway. Essentially, all our assets are outside the time lines required."

"What about NATO forces?" Jack Dehenny surprised himself by asking the question.

General Denning grunted in irritation. "I'm coming to that. We have approached both Spain and Portugal. Spain has an aircraft carrier a day's sailing from the area, which they are willing to put at the disposal of any assault force. Portugal has a very good commando unit that is being assembled and will be flown out to the carrier in the next few hours."

"And?" The president was pacing back and forth in front of the seated men like a caged lion.

"Sir?" The General seemed nonplussed.

"What do the Portuguese and Spaniards want in return?"

The General frowned. "Nothing . . . beyond the US accepting responsibility and liability for any passenger casualties and hardware."

Secretary-of-State, Max Wilson, cleared his throat. "I'm sure we'll hear from both if this is successful and perhaps even if it's not."

Ed Mason spoke flatly. "Mr. President, we cannot afford to have CANCEL killed in an assault on the island. I suspect that these people are highly professional and they'll be expecting a seaborne assault. What if they've wired the plane with explosives?"

"Damn it, Ed," The 'Mr. Director' was gone for the moment, "don't you think that is my prime concern now? What ideas do you have?"

"Diplomatic. What about the Israelis releasing some of the

Hamas prisoners in exchange for the passengers?"

The Secretary-of-State snorted: "Come on Ed, get real. You know it's been a long-standing policy of theirs never to release prisoners under threat. I've been talking to the prime minister and he is adamant; he also has unanimous cabinet backing."

"Surely, with so much at stake, we could pressure them to agree."

"We can't tell them the reason, and I doubt we have enough leverage without telling them." The secretary spread his hands in obvious frustration. "I'm just as frustrated as you are, Ed, but we don't have many options."

The president spoke sharply. "Gentlemen, with so much at stake, I want all of you to concentrate on the means of ending this crisis without delay. Jake, I want you to work with Ed closely on this. Any rivalry between the NSC and CIA can go on hold . . . you hear? I have a budget meeting in 20 minutes. Jeannie has been told that you are to have access to me at any time. You all know what's at stake." He looked at his watch. "We'll meet again at noon. Now, if you'll excuse me." He rose and left the room as the others scrambled to their feet.

Chapter 8

Day 2:   0800 hrs.

Rockland Heights – Victoria

David took another bite from the sandwiches Nigel had ordered from the housekeeper. They had no taste, and his mouth felt full of ashes. Draining his coffee, he stood up and stretched. Across the table, Rafa was pouring over the latest printouts. Obviously Colin and Laura were in the hands of a group of professional assassins. The shocking description of the death of the stewardess had blasted onto the world's news channels from the Satlink at Espargos. The Israeli Parliament had been called into emergency session and the American president had called for restraint by all sides.

Nigel put the phone down and shook his head in frustration. "If those clowns in Ottawa are telling the truth, then they've heard nothing from the Americans." For several hours Nigel had been calling friends and acquaintances in various embassies, trying desperately to find out as much information as possible. He had spent a miserable half-hour with his wife, Judith, breaking the news as gently as possible that her son and niece were in the hands of a group of terrorists.

Geoff Bayliss called to them from his seat in front of the console where he had been pouring over printouts from the TRIDENT program. "Mr. Mornay, take a look at this— perhaps it's significant."

David was at his side in two strides. Bayliss handed him a tear sheet and pointed to an item several paragraphs long which he'd circled in red felt pen. "It may be coincidental, but it's a group of Hamas rebels holding that aircraft."

David smoothed the tearsheet out on the boardroom table and read:

SENT/AP/Reuters: Sat 5 00.05am Gendis nohold

The final series of meetings between the vice chairman of the PLO and Ali Khufra, the second-in-command of Hamas, is scheduled to start today in Victoria, British Columbia. United Nations observers, one of which is Canada's UN delegate, Mike Monroe, will continue as moderators for the talks. The provincial government is host to the meeting that is being called a working holiday for the delegates. It is hoped that after the initial meetings in Ottawa, this series of talks will repair the breach caused by PLO actions against Hamas in the Gaza Strip and the West Bank. Ali Khufra has stated that this is a major attempt to reconcile major differences in philosophy. The chairman of the PLO has recently taken a hard line against Israeli government actions restricting access to Jerusalem and Jericho.

"That's right . . . I remember them arriving last night at the hotel. I didn't take much notice."

David had booked rooms for himself and Rafa at the Empress Hotel rather than stay with Nigel. He was never comfortable in the huge mansion that had been his home as a child. It had too many memories, bad memories.

"What do you think?" Rafa was reading over David's shoulder. "It's a breakaway element that has carried out the hijacking, probably with the intention of derailing these talks."

"Perhaps." A nerve was jumping in David's jaw, just under the skin. "But it's the best chance we've got. Look, I'm going down to the convention centre right away. If I can talk to someone from the delegation, perhaps they can persuade these fanatics to ease up."

"I doubt if we'll get close, and you can be sure that the media are going to be all over them. But I'll come with you."

David looked at his watch: "It's early. The media are probably not up to speed on this yet but, in any case, I can't just sit around. Nigel, are you coming?"

"Look I've called Ottawa and I'm waiting for the minister to get back to me. I think we will have more success through official channels than through any other method. I have to go up and check on Judith again, so . . . no . . . go without me. I'll monitor the incoming data until you get back." He reached for the intercom remote and, selecting a number, depressed the switch. "George, can you bring the car round?"

Chapter 9

Day 2: 8.30 am.

Empress Hotel, Victoria, B.C.

The Empress Hotel, stately, dignified and massive, is the jewel in the crown of the Fairmont hotel chain. Set back from a massive stone seawall facing James Bay and the distant blue ranges of the island interior, the hotel front overlooks carefully tended lawns and gardens that sweep down to Government Street and the wide pedestrian walkway that, in turn, overlooks the inner harbour and waterfront promenade. Built in an age when the British Empire was at its height and public and civic buildings proclaimed the greatness of its Queen Empress, everything about the hotel is massive, rising six floors from solid stone foundations resting on piles driven 125 feet to bedrock and with 30-inch thick brick walls. During an earth tremor in 1967 the only damage was a slight separation of one of the staircases.

Loud voices filled the hotel's vice regal suite where the Hamas and PLO delegates were gathered in excited conference. The news of the hijack had just been relayed to them as they were assembling prior to a tour of the 'City of Gardens' laid on by the mayor and council of Victoria.

Attached to the back of the Empress, through the old conservatory, the Victoria Conference Centre had been designed in modern fashion to blend in with the hotel; the two-storey structure in honey-coloured brick-and-green steel roofing matched the more ancient section perfectly. When David and Rafa's car arrived outside the Centre, the morning rush hour was in full swing. The part of the city that encompassed the Empress Hotel, Conference Centre and Provincial Museum was gridlocked as commuters struggled their way through a set of failed traffic lights at the junction of Belleville and Government streets. A motorcycle policeman was desperately trying to restore order. Cursing the delay as they crawled along, David directed

George to drop them off at the junction of Douglas and Belleville. Exiting the car without waiting for it to come to a full stop, which was hardly necessary as the traffic movement was so slow, David and Rafa trotted quickly across the intersection before the lights changed. David was striding so quickly that Rafa found himself unable to keep up.

"Dave, for heaven's sake slow down. I can't keep up. Your goddamn legs are longer than mine."

David slowed, but clearly he was impatient to get to the Hotel and Conference Centre as quickly as possible. "Sorry, I'm afraid that they'll be in conference soon and we'll have missed our chance."

"Dave, it's barely eight thirty. I have yet to find any bureaucrat who starts work before nine anywhere in the world." But Rafa lengthened his stride. After passing several boutiques, the two men entered the Convention Centre up two short flights of wide steps that led in from Douglas Street. At the top of the stairs they entered a large foyer. Without breaking stride, David turned right and looked for the information booth. A young woman in a dark skirt and tailored jacket smiled at them from behind a counter. Changing direction, David approached her.

"Excuse me, but where is the PLO/Hamas conference taking place?"

"Ah yes, you must be looking for the press conference. You're in the wrong building. The press conference is taking place in the Empress Hotel." She riffled some papers in front of her. "I think . . . Oh yes, it's in the vice regal room."

"Thank you. I guess we can go through the prefunction lobby into the Empress?"

"Yes, through the conservatory," she pointed, "the passage at the other side." She smiled brightly. "Have a good day."

"What! . . . Oh yes . . . thank you." David and Rafa made their way quickly across the marble floor of the prefunction lobby. David turned to Rafa with a grim smile. "What an inane comment to make on a day like today of all days."

Rafa grunted. "It's not her fault. They program these poor

kids with a set of prepared slogans. It's as much as her job is worth not to make the same comment to everyone she deals with. I guess some brain-dead idiot in advertising wrote up a set of specs 20 years ago and no one has ever evaluated how often these trite little slogans actually turn people off." They had reached the entrance to the conservatory and, ducking under an over-luxuriant hanging basket of fern, found themselves in a wide passage. Shops flanked both sides of the marble-floored passage and the decor was pure Victorian. Giant pots with exotic shrubbery lined the walls and guests in casual attire moved in and out of the open doors holding packages. From the price tags in the shop windows, this was very much an exclusive shopping area. David and Rafa ignored the people moving around them and made directly for the double bank of elevators at the end of the passage. David was reaching for the elevator call button when a quiet voice stopped him. A burly policeman in RCMP uniform stepped into their path.

"Can I help you?" He raised one eyebrow inquiringly.

Rafa cut in before David had a chance to speak. "We are guests at this hotel. What's the problem officer?"

The mountie did not answer but reached behind to lift a clipboard from a small table. "Your names please, gentlemen."

"David Mornay, Room 311, and Rafa Modesto, Room 324."

The mountie flipped a couple of sheets over and ran his finger down the list. "Ah yes, may I see some ID please, sir."

David snapped his wallet open and removed his driver's licence. Rafa pulled his pilot's licence out of his jacket. Scrutinising both photographs, the mountie nodded his thanks and handed the documents back. "A visiting delegation have just left their rooms on the fifth floor and are now on their way to tour the city with the mayor, so you should have no trouble getting to your rooms." He smiled. "I would recommend you avoid the tea lobby for a while if you want to avoid the scrum. I should warn you that there's a news conference scheduled in the vice regal room this afternoon and security will be in place for about an hour. Thank you, gentlemen." He stood aside to let them pass, but David shook his head.

"No, I think we'll take a quick look at the excitement. Come Rafa." The two men turned towards the tea lobby and, as they did so, saw a second man sitting inside an open doorway. This man did not acknowledge their presence, but his eyes never left their faces as they walked past.

"Security," David breathed, as they walked into the tea lounge and out of earshot. "I never gave a thought to how seriously the government is taking this. It's just as well we're staying here. Otherwise I'm quite sure we wouldn't have been allowed within a hundred yards of either delegation."

Rafa nodded. "After Lima and the Tupac Amaru can you blame them?"

Inside the lobby a group of men were illuminated by television lights as they made their way to the main exit. Twenty or more male and female reporters were shouting questions at the group who were surrounded by security officers. David recognised Bill Stewart from CKGU, the local station, and a smartly dressed, attractive brunette struck a chord in his memory. He had seen her on TV but couldn't remember the station. Directly ahead of them a large reporter, David guessed from one of the main papers, probably The *Globe and Mail* or *Vancouver Sun*, was asking one of the delegation a question over the heads of the security cordon and all the reporters waited for the answer. The man addressed might have been handsome had his face not been badly pitted with old acne or smallpox scars. He was dressed in a conservative suit and pale tie, his long, sleek black hair pulled back behind his ears.

"Mr. Khufra, you have heard of the hijacking of the 747 by elements of Hamas. One person has been murdered. What is your reaction to this act of piracy?"

The man smiled but his eyes glittered. "First, let me correct your statement. Hamas has nothing to do with this hijacking. We have a group claiming Hamas affiliation. We do not have any such group within our organisation." He held up his hand as two other reporters started shouting. "Having said that, I can understand the frustration that some of our wilder elements feel at Israeli intransigence. I cannot condone the unfortunate death of the stewardess—if it really has occurred—and I sincerely hope that this most unfortunate episode can be ended quickly." A pink-faced aide touched Khufra on the shoulder, he nodded and began to move out of the hotel with other members of the delegation. A reporter, hidden by the bulk of the *Globe and Mail* reporter, snapped a last question.

"Mr. Khufra, isn't it true that, in past statements you have publicly supported the use of terror, including hijacking?" David saw Khufra's head snap up and his smile disappear.

"Your information is incorrect. Now, if you'll excuse me. . . ."

The reporter, a former foreign correspondent who had much experience of politics in the Middle East, smiled and, reaching into a jacket pocket, produced a crumpled sheet of paper. Holding it towards Khufra, he asked, "This is a transcript of your remarks to the Organisation of African Unity in Addis Ababa last year. In it you are quoted as saying you will use any and all methods to achieve your objectives—including hijacking. Is that correct?"

Khufra half turned back and, for a split second his eyes met David's, and the sheer rage and hate they contained blasted across the space between them. Dar Yassin must have realised that a public relations disaster was in the making for he pulled at Khufra's arm. "We will be late, Ali; perhaps you can continue this conversation at the main press conference this afternoon." For a long moment Ali Khufra stared at the reporter before shaking his arm free of Yassin's grip, but he nodded and the two men turned to hurry after the retreating delegates.

David could only shake his head in disbelief. Rafa was pulling at his sleeve. "Amigo, quickly. We might get a word in before they leave."

"No!" David stared at the retreating backs of the delegation. He was breathing hard and the exclamation sounded harsh.

"Those bastards are in this up to their necks . . . did you see his eyes?"

"Dave, you can't judge so quickly. Hell, we only heard the end of the news conference. The poor bastard may have been under the gun for quite a time."

David turned to look at Rafa as if seeing him for the first time. "You're a good man, my friend, but I have 30 years of judging men. That one is evil, and I would lay everything I own that he and his crew know a hell of a lot more about this hijacking than they pretend." He was shaken, realizing with sudden intensity that what had been a desperate gamble, probably doomed to failure, had never been a realistic possibility, given the nature of the man he had just heard. Now the full weight of what had happened to his daughter and nephew hit him with the force of a bucket of ice water. He shivered, shaking himself. "Judas Priest, how stupid can you get?"

"Dave, Dave . . . It was worth the try . . . anything is worth trying in circumstances like these. I still think we should approach them. Be fair . . . you could be wrong."

"No . . . no . . . Rafa, I'm going up to my room. I want to spend some time alone. I need to clear my mind." He gripped Rafa's arm with a force that made the Chilean wince. "Go back to the house and monitor the incoming info. Give me a call if there are any changes in the situation. I'll take a taxi back later."

Dubiously, Rafa scanned David's face. "Look Dave, are you all right? This change in direction is very sudden."

"I'm fine. I just need time to gather my thoughts. I've tried to overcome my fears by stupid hopes . . . You understand? I need time to come to grips with this situation." He smiled, but his face looked strained and was pale. "Do this for me, my friend."

"Dave. I don't like this, but perhaps you do need some time alone. I'm going back to Nigel's, but if I don't hear from you by lunchtime I'm coming to get you . . . OK?" With a last shake of his head, Rafa reluctantly pushed his way through a group of departing journalists.

David stood for several minutes deep in thought then finally made for the main door. His mind was whirling and he felt vaguely nauseous. He needed fresh air. His fears for Laura's safety caused his hands to tremble. He walked down the steps from the verandah towards the Inner Harbour across Government Street. He felt a blind rage rising and fought it, oblivious of the stares of passersby, muttering to himself: "Bastards, all of them, being wined and dined by a bunch of bloody sycophants." He had heard the pious denial of involvement in the hijacking. Even now his daughter was being held hostage to the whims of these vicious pirates. "Bloody, bloody bastards . . . if I could have them alone for a time . . . damn them!" He slammed his hand down on the concrete wall that flanked the wharf. "I wonder how these fat cats would react to being held hostage." Suddenly the idea popped fully fledged into his mind. He could take them hostage in exchange for his daughter and Colin. He stood feet spread, both hands on the low wall, staring across the yacht basin. "No—it's too ridiculous," he told himself, logic fighting his emotions and losing. His lips pulled tight across his teeth. He must not allow emotion and tiredness to take over his common sense. He sighed deeply. "Stop kidding yourself, Dave; middle-aged men don't play at being Robin Hood." He walked back to the hotel and his room.

"And now the news—Canada's unemployment rate rose again for the fourth consecutive month. N.D.P.'s Josh Mazwell stated today that Liberal MLA, Neil Davis, is guilty of misuse of government vehicles. The South African Airways 747 hijacked last night is on the ground at the airport of Espargos in the Cape Verde Republic. Unconfirmed reports state that a stewardess has been shot by the hijackers. The Panama Canal Zone is the scene of rioting again for the third consecutive day, and here in Victoria the PLO/Hamas conference on the future of a joint approach to problems in the Gaza Strip and the West Bank will give a press conference in the Empress Hotel at noon today."

David snapped the switch off. A knock on the door interrupted

his pacing, some ten minutes later: "Put it on the table, thanks."
An exchange of hands, the bottle of Glendronach and a fresh
notepad lay on the table. The porter went off with several $20
bills crumpled in his hand. David sat at the table after filling a
glass with the 12-year-old malt. He drew the pad towards him
and began to make notes in a quick decisive hand; gradually the
plan took shape. He must snatch one man, probably Khufra:
No, one would not be enough. The hijackers held 240 people.
He needed maximum leverage, and one person would not be
sufficient. How to get them together without the security services
blocking his plans?

He was in the same hotel, so access was established. He had a
Walther P38 in his safety deposit box at the bank a few blocks
away. He had taken the weapon from the body of a North
Vietnamese officer he had killed during the vicious battle to
retake Hué; he'd cleaned and test fired it regularly. He did not
know why he had kept the weapon, then again perhaps he did.
He remembered the enemy soldier's face as the two men had
encountered each other in the shattered remains of a church.
Badly wounded, the NVA officer had swung the pistol towards
David and died as a short burst from David's submachine gun
flung him back. Picking up the pistol and finding it empty, David
stared into the slack face of his enemy and felt a terrible
weariness. These people were going to fight until the last one
was dead; they were brave and ruthless and would never give up.
He knew then that this war was unwinnable. Two weeks later,
badly wounded by a grenade, he was evacuated to Japan and
never returned to Vietnam. Kate had often chided him and
suggested he dispose of the pistol, but irrationally he felt that
he owed the NVA officer a debt. He could not bring himself to
dispose of the weapon, his personal talisman, and now he was
glad that he had not succumbed to Kate's urging.

But a pistol, even a Walther P38, might not deter a zealous
security man from attempting to rush him. He needed a threat
so dangerous that even the most foolhardy would not be tempted
to go against him. What would do? Possibly a grenade, but you

don't just purchase a grenade from the corner store. He pushed the problem from his mind, concentrating on the first move: how to capture the group.

By 10.30 a.m. the whisky bottle was, apart from the first drink, nearly full, and a pile of neatly written sheets lay in front of David. He sat for the next half hour timing first one plan then the next. Apparently satisfied, he pushed his chair back and stood up, stretching his tall frame to ease the stiffness. He picked up the telephone and, with what looked like a shopping list, began dialling various numbers around Victoria. Later, investigators would piece together a finely detailed sequence of apparently unrelated requests that individually were innocuous but, when combined, were deadly.

Through the driving rain the NVA came, their outlines blurred by the intensity of the downpour. They were totally unaware of the waiting marines lying soaked along the paddy dyke. David, grenades spread in front of him waited, beside Corporal Washington, the machine gunner. The leading Viet passed ten feet from where David lay; two more passed before the trap was sprung and automatic fire raked the double line of North Vietnamese soldiers. The man directly in front of David collapsed in slow motion as if the weight of water was driving him to his knees. David fired short bursts, then began tossing grenades towards the main cluster of the enemy. A wet smack made him turn to Washington, and he was stunned to see the machine gunner collapse with a bullet through the bridge of his nose. He rolled the body away from the gun and slid across to replace the dead marine. David swung the muzzle seeking targets, rage choking him. He and Washington had survived their first tour together, and now the skinny black soldier with the infectious grin was dead. The leading Viet had miraculously escaped the first hail of fire and, dropping to his knees, coolly returned fire, but a grenade dropping directly in front of him had blinded him and driven cast-iron fragments deep into his gut. He began to moan, his voice rising in intensity as the pain surged through the initial shock. David, his grief and anger fanned by the adrenalin released into his system, swung the machine gun across to sight in the dying North Vietnamese soldier and sent a stream of bullets whipping across the mud to slam the Viet over and into silence.

The TV, tuned to CBC had remained on throughout the time David had been planning. Now as he sat leaning back in the chair looking at the ceiling, deep in memories, a disembodied voice jerked him out of his reverie.

".....reports that a spokesman for the hijackers has stated that two cabin crew have been killed and the first passenger will be executed at midnight local time if their demand for the release of all captured Hamas guerrilla fighters is not met by that time. The aircraft is still on the ground at Ilha do Sal and no further information on the Israeli government's response is available at this time. The following pictures are very disturbing; viewer discretion is advised. We repeat, viewer discretion is strongly advised..."

David stared at the screen as a picture of a terrified stewardess came into view. A video, obviously hand held, showed a repeat of the entire sickening sequence that Captain Strydom had watched earlier. Even hardened as a combat soldier, David could not comprehend the evil he was watching. The picture changed and an obviously shaken announcer returned. . . . *"For a full news update at 12 p.m., stay tuned to this channel."* . . . The voice faded as a lissom woman, dressed in elegant evening wear and standing in a sparkling modern kitchen, smiled seductively at the camera as an advertisement for a well-known household detergent came on.

David exhaled, his hands wet with perspiration. His first thought was for Laura. Another execution was planned. What if these men felt that the execution of a little girl on worldwide TV would speed up the process of freeing their friends? Sweet Jesus! Up to the moment of the broadcast, and despite his careful planning and proposed collection of equipment, he had been hoping for an outside resolution to the crisis. Now he knew, with a sickening certainty, that no miracle would release his daughter and that, as always, he must follow his own instincts. The men he was choosing to challenge were desperate and ruthless. They would, if what he had seen and heard so far was a guide, blow themselves up with the aircraft if assaulted from the ground. He had to counter, and the only lever he might use with any chance of success was by an incredible coincidence in the same hotel with him. Now that he was committed, he felt a shiver of fear, knowing that a desperate middle-aged man should not take the world on lightly. He had always had more than his fair share of luck, but he would need far more than luck on this venture.

David collected all the notes he had made and took them into the bathroom where he tore the pages into small pieces before flushing them down the toilet. Opening the closet, he selected a dark grey shirt and lightweight jacket and slacks. His image quickly changed from that of a casually dressed tourist to that of a businessman. He pulled a lightweight raincoat over his suit and descended to the lobby where he gave his key to the desk clerk without speaking. Moving briskly, he strode out of the main doors and headed in the general direction of the downtown shopping area. His first stop was a drugstore on Douglas Street that gave him some of the ingredients he was seeking. For the next hour he collected various items until he had a large plastic bag filled to bursting. Stopping at a restaurant, he had a large bowl of clam chowder and a steak sandwich, finishing off with two cups of coffee. Checking his watch as he left the restaurant, David gave a grunt of satisfaction: he was still on time.

Returning to the hotel, he collected his key and refusing an offer of help from the attendant entered the elevator, oblivious of the other occupants. Locking his room and hanging a 'Do Not Disturb' sign on the door, he unwrapped the various parcels and set up a chemical scale on the dressing table. An hour later he washed his hands carefully and looked with satisfaction at a large lump of grey material wrapped in a clear plastic ziplok bag. He swept up the remains of various chemicals and flushed them down the toilet, thinking briefly that they would do the fish no good when they reached the ocean at the Clover Point outfall. After drying his hands, he carefully placed the plastic bag of explosive into a newly purchased black nylon camera bag. Filling the bottom half of the bag with the amorphous mass of explosive, he gently pressed it down into the corners and smoothed the top with his knuckles. He placed a thin piece of cardboard with a hole cut in the centre horizontally over the explosive. From his pocket he removed two thin one-inch-long detonators complete with attached wires. Cutting a slit in the plastic around the explosive, he pushed the detonators deep into the grey explosive through the hole in the horizontal card. He splayed the detonator wires apart above the cardboard. Removing two AAA batteries in their holder from a cheap hand calculator, he tossed the broken calculator into the wastebasket. The battery holder and its protruding wires he placed into a side pocket of the camera bag. Through a small precut hole joining the side pocket to the main bag, he drew the wires from the double AAA battery holder into the main bag. Between the detonator wires and the battery pack wires he fitted a micro switch, mounted so the toggle protruded through a small hole directly below where his hand could activate it in a second. Moving carefully, he tested the batteries separately and then tested continuity of current between the detonators and the battery holders with an 8-Range Multi–tester. Finally, double checking that the toggle switch was in the off-position, he inserted the batteries into their holder in the side pocket of the camera bag. He placed a small radio over the card and carefully zipped the lid closed. Slinging the carrying strap over his shoulder, he stood up and looked critically at himself in the full-length mirror. Satisfied, he placed the apparatus on the dressing table.

David took off his clothes and had a quick shower, letting the cold water sting his skin. He selected a dark grey suit from the wardrobe and dressed with care. He put on a plain white shirt in sea-island cotton, only the cut giving away its expensive origin to an experienced eye. He chose a silk Gucci tie in sombre blues and greys. Then he slipped into the $2,000 suit that made him look like a successful stockbroker, but a stockbroker who kept in excellent physical shape, and finally pushed his feet into casual but expensive black Italian shoes. Until his marriage to Kate, he had worn only functional clothing, but she had carefully steered him, over time, into a more civilised mode of dressing. He was wealthy in his own right, yet money had never really interested him. Apart from his lovely farm in the Fulford Valley that was the envy of his neighbours, he spent very little on himself. On the other hand, he was extremely generous with Kate and Laura and had to be continually restrained by Kate from purchasing anything new on the toy market that interested Laura. "David, it's enough she has a pony, riding ring, private riding lessons and a cupboard, big enough to park a pickup in, which is absolutely full of toys. No more please." In mock anger she had picked up the latest acquisition before Laura had a chance to see it and had swept it away to store it for a suitable occasion. Smiling at the memory, he suddenly realised where he was and what he was doing, and a flicker of pain closed his eyes. He combed his hair and, contemplating himself in the full-length mirror, he saw a tall grey-haired man who might well be attending a banker's convention. The face was pale and drawn—harsh lines cut from the nose to chin—only the eyes lifted it from the ordinary. He sighed and looked at his watch, then picked up the telephone.

"Desk, please connect me to Professor Peter Watson. He's an observer with the PLO/Hamas delegation."

"I'm sorry, sir, but the gentlemen of the United Nations and both delegations are in conference."

"I'm aware of that. Please connect me. This is urgent."

Stiffly: "Please wait."

There was a singing sound, a click, then he heard the phone ringing. "Yes?" A strong Canadian accent, probably East Coast.

"Professor Peter Watson, please."

"Who? Oh yes, hold on a second." David guessed it must be a security guard, probably RCMP, who had answered. He could hear much background noise, laughter and the clink of glasses. The phone was lifted.

"Watson here."

"Ah, Professor Watson, my name is Mornay, David Mornay. We met last year in Johannesburg at the Earlton hotel. You were giving a talk to ConAmGeo executives on the future mining prospects in Palestinian areas of the Middle East." This statement, curiously enough, as later investigators found out, was partly true. While no longer part of the ConAmGeo group since his premature retirement seven years previously, David Mornay had been in Johannesburg as a consultant for Mornay Mining and had been invited to sit in as an observer.

"Oh yes, Mr. Mornay, I recall the lecture. Whatever are you doing in Victoria? It's a long way from South Africa."

"ConAmGeo does business all over the world, professor. I must confess that I was pleasantly surprised to hear we were both in the same hotel. I was hoping to say 'hello' before going on to Vancouver."

"Of course, Mr. Mornay. What about this evening, say six? The preliminary sessions will be over by then and we can have a drink together."

"Unfortunately, professor, I'll be leaving for the airport in the next half hour and I understand that you are in conference at the moment so it seems as if I will have to pass."

"Well, that's a pity. Still, another time, perhaps."

"Yes, I'm sure we'll run across each other again . . . Oh, before I forget! I was in Stuttgart last week and attended a lecture by Professor Eisenberg on projected economic strategies for the Middle East, with particular reference to the Gaza Strip. I still have all the papers and notes with me. Perhaps they might interest you? I'll put them in an envelope and you can pick them up at the door of the conference room. It's on my way down." David waited, his heartbeat quickening; everything hinged on Watson's response.

"Well, that's very good of you, Mr. Mornay. Tell you what; come down right away, and I'll slip out for a few minutes."

"Excellent, excellent! Give me five minutes to get there. I'll see you then." David grinned wolfishly, his heart thumping but his hands rock steady. He picked up the camera case, slinging the strap over his right shoulder, and then placed the squat Walther P38, after checking the safety catch, into the wide pocket of his raincoat. He hung the raincoat over his left arm and simultaneously lifted in his left hand a slim black leather attaché case, with his Leica camera tied to its handle. He checked to see that the letter with his instructions was conspicuous on the bed. Then he left the room, locked the door, and dropped the key into his suit pocket.

Stepping into the deeply carpeted corridor he nearly collided with a cleaning woman, and froze for a second, sweat breaking out under his arms. He forced a smile and mumbled an apology. "Steady," he told himself. "Breathe smoothly, relax, it's going to work." He walked down the corridor past a group of tourists who took no notice of him.

The double doors to the vice regal suite were to his right as the elevator opened. Two plainclothes RCMP officers stood beside the doors. The larger one moved towards him.

"I'm sorry, sir, this area is restricted."

"Yes, I know. Professor Watson has agreed to meet with me here. I've just spoken with him."

"You are the person who just phoned?"

"Yes."

"Can I see some ID, sir?"

David removed his wallet with his right hand and flipped it open to show his driver's licence. The police officer leaned forward to study the photograph. Satisfied, he smiled: "Please wait, sir. I'll let him know you have arrived."

David was conscious of the scrutiny of the remaining RCMP officer, who suddenly spoke, also satisfied that this well-dressed businessman posed no threat. "Nice camera you have there. It's a Leica, isn't it?"

"Yes. Mind you, I've had it for a long time. The newer ones don't seem as solid somehow."

Before the policeman could agree, Watson came through the door. A man of medium height, carrying too much weight, his belly pulled his shirt tight above a wide leather belt. He had a bushy thatch of grey hair and a florid complexion and was smiling as he came through the door, his hand outstretched.

"Mr. Mornay, it's good to see you again." The smile faded slightly as he tried to connect the face to events of a year ago, then shrugging he continued: "It's a long way from Johannesburg."

"That's the truth, Professor, but you know us travellers." He lifted the briefcase. "I have the documents in here."

David stood with his back to the elevator and had Watson directly in front of him, blocking the large mountie's view. The large mountie relaxed: it was obvious these men knew each other. David slid his hand into the pocket of the raincoat and around the worn butt of the Walther. He pulled it clear, dropping the raincoat and briefcase away from his body, and shoved the muzzle into Watson's ample stomach.

He snapped viciously. "Don't anyone move. This is not a joke."

The two mounties were stunned by the totally unexpected move and stood frozen. David motioned them clear of Watson. "Lie down on the floor, face down, and please don't do anything stupid! This case contains enough explosive to remove half this wing from the hotel."

The mounties complied slowly, their faces registering disbelief. As they stretched out, David pulled a small water pistol from his pocket, stepped quickly up to where they lay, and sprayed a fine mist into both their down-turned faces. Both immediately collapsed and a fragrant smell, similar to the odour of ethyl chloride, filled the air.

"My God, what have you done? What do you think you're doing?" Watson babbled, his face going pale.

"Pick up my briefcase, quickly now." David waited until Watson complied. "Now walk back into the conference room ahead of me, and don't call out or I'll shoot you in the back."

Watson pushed the door open, followed by David, who pressed the barrel savagely against the man's spine. Watson stumbled back into the room he had left so confidently a few minutes before.

The room was approximately 40 feet long by 20 wide. A rose-coloured, deep-pile carpet stretched unbroken from wall-to-wall. The ceiling, at least ten feet high, was painted in the same golden cream as the walls. The longest wall was broken by three sets of huge windows, separated by square columns. Each column held delicate twin golden-wall sconces that were duplicated on the opposite wall of the room. From the centre of the ceiling a golden six-branch chandelier illuminated the room and, suspended from hidden valances, heavy curtains in flowered brocade hung from ceiling to floor.

Scattered around the room were comfortable sofas and deep upholstered chairs; low tables in gleaming dark wood had been pushed against the walls to make room for the occupants.

David stood to one side of the door, keeping the pistol trained on Watson while he used his left hand to lock the door. Aware that very little attention was being paid to their entrance, he swung the pistol away from Watson's body into full view of the assembly. A woman reporter from the *Daily Colonist* spotted the pistol and her scream brought sudden and complete silence to the room.

"Please do not move. Attached to my body is a kilo of high explosive. If it's detonated, this room will cease to exist. You all remember Oklahoma city." He motioned gently with the pistol at the stunned group. "All newspaper and media people will move across to that corner." He pointed with the pistol. "Quickly, please; I'm not a patient man."

"What's this all about?" a correspondent named Riley asked.

David looked at him briefly before resuming his scan of the room. "Be quiet! I do not want any talking, don't distract me."

"But. . . ." Riley grunted in pain as a hard elbow swung by Paul Kent of *Reuters* smacked into his back.

"Shut up, you fool; he's not joking." Kent had been on the ground in Beirut when troops tried to storm the hijacked Windward Airlines jumbo. He could still see the huge explosion blow the aircraft into a ball of blazing metal and hear Carstairs of the BBC give a disbelieving gasp. "Oh my God, they've killed everyone." The final count had been 212 passengers and six

Muslim Liberation Front men. The knowledge that this cold, hard faced man carried explosives turned his stomach over.

David had not expected the large group of reporters and wanted them out of the way quickly. No sound came from outside the door: the mounties would be unconscious for another ten minutes.

"The rest of you lie down, face down."

Ali Khufra grunted in anger and made as if to walk towards David.

"Down, dog, or I'll blow your knees off." David snarled savagely, his anger barely under control.

Startled by the raw violence in Mornay's voice, Khufra hesitated, and the Russian UN delegate, Kuchinsky, caught his arm. Kuchinsky shook his head. The UN delegates and the Hamas/PLO group were now thoroughly cowed and began to lie down. The only sound breaking the silence was the frightened sobbing of a woman reporter standing with her colleagues in the opposite corner.

"You lot sit down," David pointed at the media people. Watson had not moved since entering the room and stood like a statue, uncertain of what to do next. He decided not to do anything. His mind was like a rabbit's when confronted by a cobra—frozen numb. David pointed to Paul Kent. "Come here. I need a wise man." His body tight with tension, Kent moved across the carpet towards the door.

"Take my attaché case from the professor and open it."

Kent snapped the locks open and found himself looking at a whole series of quarter-inch nylon cord cut onto four-foot lengths.

"Tie up everyone except the newspeople. Start with Scarface and tie them well. I'll check the knots myself."

Kent began with Khufra, as instructed. His mind was racing. How would this maniac manage to check each delegate? It might be possible to leave a few ropes reasonably loose and give them a chance. David did not appear to notice. Kent was tying the hands of the second delegate when David spoke again.

"If I find any loose bindings, I'll shoot you and then have

one of your colleagues start over. Don't think of being clever."

Kent stiffened his spine; his hands were slippery with sweat and he could not stop them shaking. Paul Kent was not a coward, but covering the world's hot spots for the best part of two decades had eaten away at his courage like acid dripping on limestone. Too many of his friends had made the mistake of misjudging a situation. He wiped his hands on his pants and carried on tying up the delegates firmly, thoughts of resistance fading rapidly.

It was still quiet outside the door. The two mounties had not been discovered, but David was racing against time. "OK, listen, all you media types. You will leave this room in single file. Outside the door you will find two unconscious RCMP men. You will drag them away, and, once you have cleared the area, no one is to attempt re-entry." He paused and took a deep breath. "My daughter who is six years old is on the hijacked South African Airways 747. These men," he waved the pistol at the bound delegates, "I believe are directly or indirectly responsible for that operation and, despite their denials, they support and encourage the thugs that hold the aircraft. You will advise the hijackers through your communication network that I now hold their political leaders. I will take steps to execute the entire leadership of both factions unless all the passengers are released immediately." His voice was calmer now; the hand holding the Walther was rock steady, and the feverish light had faded from his eyes. "Also advise the authorities that this bomb can be activated in a second. Any attempt by the security or police forces to storm this room will cause me to activate this device. I have no illusions about the kind of evil thugs holding my daughter. I want them to have no illusions about me." He kicked Watson behind the knee and pushed sharply. The professor fell heavily to his knees. David raised the pistol and placed the barrel at the base of Watson's neck, looking grimly in Kent's direction.

Watson croaked in a throaty whisper, his voice thick with terror: "Please . . . please don't."

Paul Kent gasped out, "I believe you . . . For God's sake man,

I don't need convincing . . . . please let him live. If you kill him,
you're no better than they are." For a long second, while nobody
dared breathe, nothing happened. Then David smiled grimly
and lowered the automatic.

"Do not attempt any foolish actions on your way out. Form
a single line. Yes, you in the blue shirt, you lead—now go."

Hesitantly at first, the group began filing out of the room,
moving more quickly as the numbers decreased. Kent continued
tying up the last of the delegates. He stood up as the last of the
newspeople exited the room.

"If you wish us to advise the hijackers of your demands, you
should at least tell us your name."

David had half turned to cover both the door and any
movement by the bound delegates. The Walther was level with
Kent's mid-section. "Are you finished?"

"Yes, look . . . I sympathise with your predicament . . . But
this won't work, you know." He raised his shoulders. "I have
seen . . . Hijackers aren't rational."

The overhead fluorescent lighting glinted dully on the barrel
of the Walther. David's face was expressionless.

"I could kill you now to prove I'm not rational either."

Kent sucked his breath in sharply, but even as his body went
cold, and an involuntary shiver passed through him, he picked
up the operative word, 'could'. This lunatic would not kill him
yet. He held his breath.

David tossed a key attached to a plastic tag. "I want you to go
to my room. On my bed is an envelope with instructions. Give
it to the police." He smiled grimly at the relieved reporter. "It is
unsealed. Read it, then seal it. I will know in a short time if you
have followed my instructions. Remember this: all their lives,"
here David gestured with the pistol at all the bound delegates,
"are hanging on a very thin thread and depend on strict adherence
to my instructions. Now, go!" The eyes were bleak again, and
Kent could see a nerve twitch in the taut muscles of Mornay's
face.

Kent stepped through the doors into the corridor, his heart

pounding. He saw two city police officers crouching with guns drawn at the end of the corridor where it made a sharp turn. Shaking his head and silently mouthing the word, 'no', Kent moved towards them in a crouching run. He knew he must get to a telephone. What a story—hot damn! Now that he was clear he reverted automatically to being a newspaperman. A police officer stepped back around the corner with him.

"What's happening? Who else is coming out?"

"No one. I'm the last reporter. He made me tie up all the delegates then told me to go." Kent placed his hand on the policeman's arm. "Don't try to get in. He has a bomb and he'll use it."

"Yes, we know. The others told us. Can you describe the device?"

"Are you bomb squad?"

"No. They're coming, but tell me everything you remember, especially the details."

"The bomb is in a camera bag, the type used for carrying spare lenses, camera bodies and such. There is a switch protruding from the side of the bag. It must be attached to a detonator. He claimed to have a kilo of high explosive in the case and warned us to remember the Oklahoma bombing."

"Do you think he's bluffing?" The sergeant, a 20-year veteran of the city force, had seen and heard many queer things in his time, but this took the cake. A hijack in Victoria and at the staid old Empress of all places.

"I'm absolutely certain he's deadly serious, but I sure as hell don't want to find out the hard way." He tried to push past the two policemen but was restrained by a large hand on his chest.

"Hold on, not so fast! We need all the information you can remember. It's going to become very important shortly."

"Look, sergeant, there were ten of us in there. Don't you think it would be better to have us questioned as a group? Let's find a room where you can speak to all of us?"

The policeman scowled; he did not need gratuitous advice on top of a bomb threat. "All the other media people are being questioned in the lobby. Join them and don't leave the hotel until you're told."

Kent nodded: "Of course." He walked casually to the stairs and, as he turned the corner, heard the policeman talking into his radio. "Last media person on his way dow . . ." Once out of sight, he broke into a fast trot, heading for Mornay's room. He found it quickly and, inserting the key into the lock pushed, the door open. The room was tidy, bed made, and on the bed cover Kent saw a large manilla envelope. Gingerly he picked it up and noted that, as David had said, it was unsealed. Inside were several sheets of ruled paper, the type used by schoolchildren as fillers in their folders. He drew them out carefully and sat on the bed to read. The instructions were in a neat fast hand and he whistled softly when he saw the underlined deadline. Reaching for the room phone, he dialled quickly. "Frank? Don't say anything, just listen carefully and copy everything. Ready? . . . Good! Here goes . . ."

Chapter 10

Day 2:   1200 hrs. Victoria/1800 hrs. Espargos.

Ilha do Sal – Espargos Airfield

Captain Strydom listened incredulously to the message coming through his headset. "My God, it's unbelievable." He swung his head to watch the reaction of the hijacker with the craggy face who called himself Davis. This man who had orchestrated the killing of two of his crew was undoubtedly the leader of the entire group—both the air and land-based hijackers. The Swede, if that's what he was, removed his headset and his face was drained of colour.

"You are under no circumstances to discuss this with the passengers. Is that understood?" His eyes fixed on a hijacker in camouflage guarding the door to the cockpit. "Fetch Kassim and O'Doull." His voice rasped and the hijacker stiffened and ducked through the curtain.

They waited and Strydom felt the first stirring of hope begin to surge in what after the killings, he had considered a hopeless situation. He had realised then that these men were not going to let anyone live, no matter what the Israelis did. Why were they so free with each other's names? No attempt had been made to hide the faces of the executioners and evidently they were not afraid of reprisals as there were to be no survivors.

Kassim entered first, followed by O'Doull. Without preamble, Davis grated, "Early this morning a man captured all the political leaders of both Hamas and the PLO. As you know, they were attending the conference on forming a unified front. He is now holding them hostage in Victoria, Canada."

This would be comic, Strydom thought, if it were not so serious. He saw the same stunned incredulity sweep across the Arab's face. "He demands," Davis continued, "the immediate and unconditional release of all passengers. It appears we have a member of his family aboard."

"No." Kassim almost shouted the word, his cocky arrogance dissolving under the shock. "We cannot, we must not, it is a trick."

The Swede stared at him, the cold eyes unblinking. Privately, he wondered how much stress the men under his command would stand. "Yes, it might be, but I suspect not. Still, you are right; we need proof and time to think." He rubbed a hand over his jaw slowly. "Tell Wahid and Khalil, but, for the time being the men must not be told."

Still in shock, Kassim moved out the door. Davis turned to O'Doull. "Warn the men to keep their hands off the passengers—yes, I know what I said before, but that order is rescinded. Now more than ever we may need them." He turned to Strydom and smiled coldly. "Don't raise your hopes too high, captain. If this is a trick, we'll double the number of passengers shot every fifteen minutes. I want our men freed by midnight."

"*Your* men?" interjected Strydom. "Good God, man, you are European! This is an Arab-Israeli fight. What are you involved for? The others I can understand, but . . ."

"Enough. . . ." The eyes were as flat as sanded agate. "Enough captain! My reasons are my own." Turning, he rapped out an order in fast Arabic to the guard who had returned to his position by the door. The man nodded and moved forward on the flight deck, fingering his weapon. "This man, captain, has orders to shoot you if you attempt to do anything other than sit until I get back. It's time to meet the passenger who has caused all the trouble: a young lady, the message said." He smiled at nothing in particular and then walked out of the cockpit into the upstairs cabin where the flight deck and cabin crew were being guarded by several hijackers. As he drew near, a stocky dark-skinned Arab hijacker in faded camouflage stood up and asked softly, "What do we do now, sir?"

"Wait until midnight. By then all our comrades should be free."

"I mean about the execu . . ."

"Postponed until further orders."

"Yes, sir." Davis fancied the Arab was pleased and it surprised him.

"What about the capture of . . .?" Davis shook his head and shot a warning glance in the direction of the other hijackers. "First they must prove it is true. We have other plans—at all costs keep this from the men until I tell you it's OK."

"But what if . . . ?"

The stone face smiled, and the effect was startling. Confidence and power poured from this man. He shook the Arab's shoulder gently. "Khalil, Khalil, do you think we did not expect trouble? It is a great prize we fight for also," and now the banter was gone from his voice. "You are a soldier and I expect you to obey orders. Enough of this talk."

The hijacker, Khalil, nodded but his face was still troubled. He was an experienced Hamas guerilla fighter, having pitted his skills against the Israeli Army since the late 70's. The fact that he was still alive and wanted by one of the most efficiently competent security forces in the world was a tribute to his ability. He had been chosen for his calmness under fire and his ability to control the widely divergent personalities under his command, but he lacked the administrative ability that makes a superior leader. For this operation he had been placed as second in command to Kassim by the Central Committee. It was a position he resented, but he was careful to conceal his feelings.

Impassively, Davis watched Khalil move down the stairs. If Khalil was worried, the others would fall apart. Davis knew he must, at all costs, prevent that happening. Again he stroked his jaw reflectively. He pointed at a pretty young flight attendant trying to be as unobtrusive as possible by sitting behind the bulk of the First Officer. "Come here, Miss."

Casting a despairing glance over her shoulder in the vain hope that Davis did not mean her, she responded. "What . . ," swallowing and then clearing her throat, "what is it you want . . . sir."

Davis looked at her and did not reply for a long moment. He knew what was going through her head. Two of her companions had been dragged away and shot. Was she to be the next? She had been trained to deal with almost any emergency, but this frightening reality had rendered her helpless.

"Take me to these passengers." He looked at the piece of paper in his hand. "Miss Laura Mornay and Colin Mornay."

"I'll have to get the passenger list." Her hands shook so much that she had to cross her arms and clamp them tightly against her body.

"Well, do so."

Five minutes later Davis walked behind the stewardess towards the seat where Laura was stretched out, her little head resting on Colin's lap. Colin sat staring out the window and turned his head to watch Davis approach.

The Swede stopped in the aisle. He gazed down at the sleeping Laura and muttered softly to himself. "So you are the cause of all our trouble."

Colin felt his stomach turn to ice. He had not seen the executions from where he sat, but he had heard the whispered shock of those who had. Carefully, so as not to wake Laura, he slid sideways, laying her head on the seat. He rose to his feet, blocking the terrorist's view of the child. He faced Davis in the aisle. "What do you want? She's just a little girl."

Davis studied the well-built young man in front of him. He did not smile, but his voice was pleasant. "You must be Colin Mornay—and that must be Laura. Wake her up. I want you both to come with me." He turned and started back the way he had come.

Colin felt his knee begin jumping. It always did when he was nervous. "Why?" His voice cracked slightly. Davis stopped and turned around slowly. He frowned.

"We can discuss that upstairs—now come."

Colin hesitated. He was not a coward, but right now his mind was in turmoil. Realising that he had no choice, he lifted Laura gently and carried the child, who stirred and grumbled, then promptly fell asleep again, tucking her head into his chest as he climbed the stairs into the business class lounge. From the top of the stairs he saw some of the air and cabin crew in the front seats. Several passengers who seemed more important to the hijackers than the others were sitting at the rear of the lounge. They had bruises and one had a badly cut lip; obviously they had been beaten. Colin felt a shiver run through him. Jesus, what if they started hurting Laura? Suddenly, terrible rage flooded through his six-foot frame and he knew with absolute certainty that he would die to protect her.

Davis indicated seats away from both groups, and Colin slid into the window seat, still cradling Laura.

"Where is your uncle?"

Colin's astonishment was too real to be faked. "My uncle?"

"Yes, where is he right now?"

Colin stared at Davis. His brain was racing, what did this man want? He tried to stall. "Why do you want to know?"

"Mornay, don't try my patience. I know where he is. I simply require confirmation."

"Then you don't need me to tell you."

Davis' hand flicked like a striking snake and Colin's head rocked back, his cheek showing the livid marks of Davis' fingers. Laura started to cry. "Understand me. If you don't answer quickly and honestly, I will have one of the cabin crew," he gestured to some who had risen to their feet at the sound of the slap, "taken out and shot right now."

Colin sat stunned, tears of hot anger springing to his eyes. He shook his head, fighting the rage and frustration that surged in conflicting currents through his frame. Calming Laura, he finally looked up and stared into the colourless eyes of the man facing him. "In Victoria, British Columbia."

"What does he do for a living?"

"He is semi-retired but does consulting work. He's a mining engineer."

"Why are you and his daughter on this plane?"

Simply and quickly, his gaze never wavering from the Swede's face, Colin explained about Kate's death and the subsequent events that had led to his replacing David on the trip to South

Africa at the last minute.

"Shrapnel, you said. Where was he wounded?" Davis leaned forward intently.

"Vietnam, a place called Hooey. There was a big battle."

Davis' face paled and he was no longer looking at Colin but into some dark night of his own. "Hué . . . you mean Hué, the old Imperial capital on the Perfume River . . . so—we have something in common." He shook his head and focussed back to Colin. "Why did he fight for the Americans . . . He is a Canadian . . . Why?"

Colin shook his head, "I don't know why . . . My parents would never talk about it . . . the reasons why he left home I mean."

"You said he is a mining engineer. Does he handle a lot of explosives?"

Colin looked nonplussed, "I don't know . . . not since the war, I guess. He is more into construction management, but he was an explosive expert in the Marines."

Davis stood up and laced his fingers behind his back. He stretched his shoulders and exhaled a deep sigh. "A damned marine . . . of all the bloody people . . ." He stared down at Colin, his face expressionless. "Stay here . . . I will need you again."

Colin nodded. "Why is all this important to you? My uncle is not in politics."

"Really! Well he's into politics now. Your uncle, young Colin, has just completed a hijack of his own."

Colin stared at him with total disbelief in his eyes. "What are you talking about? He's due to go into hospital."

"I mean, that your uncle has managed to imprison a group of men he believes are connected to our struggle. He demands that we release all the passengers in return for the safety of his hostages."

Colin's jaw dropped, then his face changed and a slow smile started. "Holy shit . . . way to go, Dave!" He looked at the impassive face watching him, "What are you going to do?"

Before Davis could answer, the Arab called Khalil strode quickly down the aisle towards them. "Colonel, please come."

With only a brief, "Stay in your seat and do not talk to the others," Davis turned and followed Khalil down the spiral staircase.

Colin hugged Laura to stop his hands from shaking. He felt a huge surge of hope that they were going to make it.

Chapter 11

Day 2: 1300 hrs.

Empress Hotel Victoria B.C.

David finished checking the bound delegates. He tightened several that Kent either deliberately or in his fear failed to secure properly. None of the delegates was disposed to argue with him, for he placed the muzzle of the pistol behind each delegate's ear while he checked the bonds. Only Khufra had tried to twist under the hard knee in his back. He now lay unconscious from a butt stroke to the temple.

"Do you really believe the hijackers will free your daughter?" Ali Al-Azhar asked in a level voice. He pushed himself into a sitting position with his back against the wall.

David smiled without humour. "Your life depends on it."

"You cannot kill innocent people to right an injustice to yourself." Peter Watson was still in shock from his brush with death but he could not stop himself blurting out the words that roared round his brain.

"I have no intention of killing innocent people, Watson. You see, I don't consider any of you innocent." He turned to look around the room. The locked door was secure. The height of the room above the ground outside would make an external assault difficult, but David knew what he was up against. The Canadian government would mobilise their resources and his only hope was that fear of the terrible consequences of a bomb detonating in a small room would stay their hand. He had judged to a hair the reaction of the Reuters' reporter, Kent. Forcing Watson to his knees and threatening to shoot him in the first few minutes of the hostage taking had been a risky gamble, but Kent had swallowed the ploy fully. Now Kent would be telling all who would listen that David Mornay was fully capable of carrying out his threat to detonate the device.

Kuchinsky and Monroe, the other two members of the UN

team, had copied Al-Azhar's example and now sat with their backs to the wall, their hands pulled awkwardly behind them. Monroe was recovering from his initial shock, and deep anger was beginning to build. He was a proud man, and it was a personal affront to have this happen in Canada of all places and worst of all in Victoria where the delegates had come at his instigation. He was not afraid, but he was shrewd enough to see in this big grey-haired man with the pale blue eyes a very dangerous specimen. He decided to keep a civil tongue in his head until he could find a way of resolving this mess.

Abu Hakim, the PLO vice-chairman, and Ahmad, his assistant, were clearly frightened. Abu Hakim, because Mornay's accent puzzled him. Influenced by so many years away from Canada, David's accent was now an amalgam of Canadian/American/ South African tones. It sounded almost, but not quite, like that of a certain Israeli general whom Abu Hakim had met during the peace talks in Ramallah. So he assumed that David must be an Israeli Secret Service officer who might well be aware of the role that he had played a mere two weeks before in having a group of trained insurgents shipped through Turkey to the Chechen Republic. Now he waited while fear twisted his stomach and brought an uncontrollable tic to his eye.

Ahmad was afraid simply because he was a coward, a politician who preached peace to the world and war to his select cadres, an opportunist with unbounded ambition. Ahmad had built a reputation of stern moral rectitude by following the fundamentalist faith rigidly, but rumours suggested that his private life left much to be desired. He had been sleeping badly of late and now felt that he had been given a subconscious premonition. Ahmad was certain that this hard-faced man was going to kill them all and the thought made him sick.

Khufra began to groan, his open but unfocussed eyes staring at the ceiling. The blow he had received would have kept any other man unconscious for much longer. David watched him carefully, for he considered Khufra the most dangerous of all the hostages.

Ali Khufra was an enigma to many. His cruelty was a byword

among the fighters he controlled and he had little difficulty in maintaining the harsh discipline required from his men. He was himself without fear, a legacy from his Saracen ancestors to whom war was a sport, and concealed his cunning with a mask of impassive indifference. Enemies often realised too late that what they took for stupidity was camouflage, and they paid dearly for their miscalculation. Dar Yassin, the political leader of Hamas, had discovered his protégé's talents in the grim years of the 80's, a time when internecine strife racked the party and bombings and assassinations were common. Yassin had used Khufra several times to remove rivals, in his climb to power, and had rewarded him with general command of the units in the field. It had been a shrewd move, for within 18 months Khufra had stopped squabbling within the ranks, improved discipline, and changed tactics from confrontation with the security services of Israel to savage isolated attacks on tourists. This had forced the Israeli government to spread its already overstretched security forces further, and the fear Khufra's tactics engendered slowed the flow of hard information to a trickle.

But recently Dar Yassin had perceived that all the credit Ali Khufra had received was gradually undermining his own position within the party and he had decided to dispose of him at the earliest opportunity. He watched him with a speculative look on his face as the Hamas chief of staff tested his bonds.

Both men were ruthless, but Dar Yassin, small, smooth, and a dedicated fundamentalist, was expected by many to replace Yasser Arafat as head of a single Palestinian entity, although the more moderate Arafat had a greater following within the country. Most Mid-East watchers foresaw a period of infighting that Yassin intended to win.

The other four Arabs, two from each party, made no effort to complain or argue. They made themselves as comfortable as their bonds would allow and waited for decisions from their respective leaders.

David paused to consider how long he could hold this group and he checked the windows and doors for any sign of movement outside. He was only slightly surprised at the ease with which he had captured the delegates; for all of his adult life, he had been aware that only those who dared ever succeeded. Most people only dreamt great dreams but made no attempt to put in the effort required to achieve them.

Someone spoke and David turned from his survey of the room. "And what, sir, must we call you?" The man gave a short cough. "It is easier to discuss, er . . . problems with someone who has identity."

David looked at the Sudanese UN observer and was impressed with the swarthy Arab's composure.

Watson spat out in a rush, "He's an Israeli agent, his name is Mornay, David Mornay, or is that another invention . . . another lie?"

"Lie, Professor?" David raised his eyebrows fractionally. "After reading some of your apologist writings I don't think you can call anyone else a liar." He turned away from Watson and looked directly at the Sudanese. "You now have my name. I know Khufra, Yassin, Ahmad and Watson. Now perhaps you will enlighten me as to your name and the names of your colleagues."

Al-Azhar inclined his head. "My name is Ali Al-Azhar and I am the representative of Sudan to the United Nations. Over there," he pointed with his chin, "is . . ."

"Nyet, nyet." The Russian shook his head vigorously.

"Why not Viktor? He will have our names soon enough. Did you not see the pocket radio? My Russian associate is Viktor Kuchinsky from the UN observer group. Over there is Mike Monroe, Canada's UN representative; he is the chairman of our group."

"And what is the purpose of your group?"

"Our function is to observe and assist the talks between Hamas and PLO. We were," here he smiled thinly, "the only parties acceptable to both sides."

David took a silver flask from a side pocket in the attaché case and had a quick drink. Wiping his mouth with the back of his hand, he screwed the top back on the flask. "Well, well . . ., fascinating! . . . an ex-communist, a fundamentalist, and a man from a country that can't make up its mind about anything."

"Tell me, Mr. Mornay, what will you have achieved if the hijackers of the South African aircraft refuse to release their passengers and you carry out your threat to kill us all?"

"Al-Azhar . . ., if that occurs, it will not matter to either of us. But, if it makes you feel better I'm certain that there are men in this room who are very important to the hijackers and I know they will deal."

"They will not." All eyes swung to Dar Yassin who had also pushed himself into a sitting position. "Don't believe that the hijackers represent us in any way. They are only one of many groups striving for justice in the occupied lands."

"In that case, Yassin, you'd better prepare to die." David stroked his cheek with the barrel of the pistol. "Last year I was asked to do an assessment of a mining claim in Northern Israel. There I met a man from a nearby kibbutz whose wife and five-year-old son had been abducted by Hamas guerrillas several months previously. When the bodies were discovered they had both been tortured severely; the child had both hands, feet and genitals cut off. It was done, I suspect, to put fear into the people of the kibbutz . . . and, of course, to bring justice to the people of the occupied lands."

"That sounds very much like Israeli propaganda. Our organisation does not make war on women and children."

David continued almost as if Yassin had not spoken. "Twenty-four hours later, an Israeli special forces unit ambushed the group responsible. Those who survived were interrogated by Israeli security and confessed to the two murders. They were under the direct orders of Khufra; it was his brainchild to attack the most vulnerable and to mutilate and torture children." David's eyes swept the room, and no one spoke. "So you see, Yassin, of all the men in this room you and Khufra have the least chance of surviving. Only my daughter's safe release will keep you alive."

Mike Monroe interjected. "Surely, Mr. Mornay, you realise that peace in Israel and the surrounding countries is what we are striving for. This series of meetings was organised to get a consensus that would help solve the problem."

"Really?" The contempt that he had used on Watson was back in his voice. "And the hijacking is just a gentle prod in that direction, is it?"

Monroe suppressed his anger and in a carefully modulated tone murmured, "I hardly think the UN was party to a hijacking."

David looked at him coldly. "For once I agree with you. The UN couldn't organise a piss-up in a brewery, but I bet my bottom dollar they won't fall over themselves condemning it." Before he could continue, the phone rang, a soft purr. David picked up the receiver in his left hand, the pistol in his right covering the door. "Yes?"

"My name is Nichols, Inspector Nichols of the RCMP. I will be your contact from now on, Mr. Mornay."

"I see."

"We have read your instructions and noted that you will only communicate via this telephone. Perhaps you would reconsider. I would like to talk to you face-to-face."

"You have notified the hijackers of my demands?"

"Yes, we are waiting for a reply."

"When you have their reply call me again. Also advise them I will not be patient."

"Surely, Mr. Mornay, you realise the difficulty of conducting negotiations by telephone. Please let me come up and speak to you."

"Nichols, you have very clear instructions; follow them. Any attempt to deviate from them or any attempt to free the hostages will result in disaster. Is that clear?"

"Yes, quite clear. I'll call you back shortly."

David replaced the phone, his face sombre. "I hope for all your sakes that they are not under the illusion I'm bluffing." Placing a small transistor radio on the table, he laid alongside it a cellular telephone taken from the briefcase. He hooked an earplug into his ear and plugged the cord into the transistor.

"This little unit is the latest in communications technology. I can hear newscasts, also police and other frequencies." He looked down at the huddled group without expression. "We should know your fate shortly."

Looking at the group of hostages, he wondered if they fully understood the danger they faced. The hijackers held his daughter . . . his Laura. His anger began building, and he remembered bitterly his tours of duty in Vietnam where, despite the sacrifice and courage of his brothers-in-arms, a generation of young men had been needlessly sacrificed by the stupidity of the military and political high command. He had decided then that never again would his future be dictated by fools. He had completed a mining engineering degree and joined an international mining company. He had volunteered for the most remote postings and, for a long time, had walked a lonely and self-contained path. While supervising the construction of the Tsamma Uranium plant in Namibia, he'd met Kate Richardson. Kate . . . Oh shit! . . . He squeezed his eyes shut for a second . . . had been the turning point in his life and slowly, with patience, had made him whole again. When Laura was born the protective shell around his emotions shattered and he wanted nothing more from life than to see his daughter grow and blossom. Despite the fact his brother was one of the most powerful men in Western Canada, he and Kate kept a very private life, avoiding the social whirl of the city. David was virtually unknown within his brother's government and business circles and preferred to avoid any associations that were not absolutely necessary. David trembled, a cold sweat breaking out on his face. These bastards mustn't for a moment think he was bluffing.

Chapter 12

Washington D.C.

The president of the United States sat down heavily, simultaneously motioning the others to sit. He spoke into a desk phone. "Jeannie, no interruptions—absolutely none." He spun his chair back to face the three men. "Ed, what have you got? When did the second hostage-taking occur?"

Ed Mason leaned over to lift a slim file from the lap of Jack Dehenny, deputy director of the CIA. He ran his finger down the first sheet. "It happened at 1.05 p.m. PST, that's 4.05 our time. A man carrying an explosive device overpowered guards at the PLO/Hamas conference in Victoria and is now holding 14 delegates and UN personnel hostage. He's demanding the release of the SAA jumbo or he threatens to kill off his hostages at the same rate as the hijackers kill their hostages . . ."

"Where the hell is Victoria?" This from the secretary of state.

"About 60 miles north of Seattle . . ."

"Enough, enough, you can have a geography lesson later," the president interrupted irritably. "Go on, Ed. What do we know about this man? Is it an Israeli team?"

"No, sir, that was our first assumption, but this man has nothing to do with the Israelis. He has a daughter on the aircraft." Here Mason drew a deep breath. "He was one of our . . ."

"What!" The president reared up out of his seat, both hands gripping the edge of his desk. "One of ours! Are you telling me we have a rogue agent? You said he was one of ours, was . . . Jesus man, do you realise what this means."

Ed Mason shook his head vigorously. "No, he's not an agent. He fought for us in Nam. He came from a wealthy Canadian West Coast family and volunteered for the marines in '66." Ed Mason looked at the president with distaste. The president's record as a draft dodger was public knowledge, while Mason had received the wounds to his face in the secret war against the communists in Laos. He paused as the president sank back into his seat. "There's more. He did three tours, was recommended for the Medal of Honour after the battle for Hué but refused to accept the award." There was a collective intake of breath. One did not refuse the Medal of Honour, America's highest decoration for valour.

"Why—why did he refuse—what reason did he give?"

Looking at a similar file on his lap, General Denning spoke quietly: "He gave none. His combat team took very heavy casualties, and he was severely wounded. He refused evacuation until the last of his men's bodies had been recovered. He suffered severe psychological trauma and spent several months recovering. Honourably discharged on Nov 17th, 1969." Denning looked up at both the president and Ed Mason. "This man was a very good soldier. His record is extraordinary."

"Post-traumatic stress; he's gone over the edge?" The president looked from face to face.

Jack Dehenny shook his head. "Our psycho/OP people think it's possible but unlikely. After Vietnam, he took a civil engineering degree at Berkeley, joined a European company called ConAmGeo and spent the next 25 years working all over the world. Everything we could get out of ConAmGeo at short notice indicates he was an excellent employee with no record of mental illness. Quite the contrary, he's highly regarded as being solid as a rock. I spoke to the president of ConAmGeo 20 minutes ago, and he's stunned; says this behaviour is totally out of character." Here he lifted an orange sheet of glossy paper. "This fax arrived as I was preparing to come here. It appears that Mornay—that's his name, David Mornay—lost his wife in a car crash three weeks ago. Apparently he took the news badly and was intending to travel with his daughter to South Africa when a piece of shrapnel was discovered in his neck. It was due for removal today. We're chasing this aspect; it may have some bearing on what has happened."

The president looked at Ed Mason inquiringly: "What reaction from the hijackers to this news?"

"Nothing so far. There's been a total blackout from Sal since they were advised of the hostage taking. Satellite photos show no change to the aircraft. It's still 10 hours to their deadline."

"And what about the assault team on the Spanish carrier? I'm beginning to feel like the meat in a sandwich. We're going to be damned if we do and damned if we don't. Wait . . .!" The president held up his hand. "What are the chances that the men at this conference have links to the hijacking—have you done any analysis on that scenario?"

Ed Mason flipped two pages over in his file. "We have had a crisis team analysing all the possibilities since this thing first broke. From what we have so far, there's no apparent reason for Hamas to carry out this hijack. The meetings in Canada are to try to reconcile their differences, not exacerbate them. We are tracking everything we can, but maybe Hamas is telling the truth when they claim it's a wildcat operation. Whoever planned this is either incredibly lucky or has a very good idea of our force dispersal. This damn island is the only hole in our coverage outside the present area of our Atlantic fleet, and that's too much of a coincidence. What bothers me a lot is the sophistication of this operation; it stinks of very high-level planning. I keep coming back to Iraq or Iran for the needed support."

"General?" The president turned to General Denning.

"The assault team is on the carrier and they are heading towards Sal. They will be in a position to launch a rescue in about 12 hours." General Denning ran a hand through stiff short grey hair. "We're going to use some new weapons and techniques in an attempt to minimise casualties. A Harrier from Larbruch is on the way to rendezvous with the carrier."

"And what about CANCEL'S mission?"

Ed Mason pulled his shoulders back. He ached with tiredness. "We still have more than 54 hours to execution. We have two possibilities: either this man, Mornay, pulls it off—which is highly unlikely—or the assault team manages to free the hostages without too many casualties. Either way we have to wait out the next few hours."

The president growled deep in his throat. "I don't like waiting,

Ed. Get those highly paid computer geniuses in Langley to come up with some alternate options in the next three hours. Get on to the Canadians and see what they have."

_____

Ottawa - Canada

The personal secretary to the solicitor general pushed a button on her desk.

"Yes?"

"Mr. McUlroy and Mr. Benson are here to see you, Ma'am."

"Ask them to come in."

McUlroy entered first, the thinning grey hair cut short. He looks like a policeman, the solicitor general thought. She wondered irrelevantly if she looked like a solicitor general, and what does a solicitor general look like anyway? Benson was a much younger man, in his late 30's, the solicitor general guessed. She glanced at the briefing notes: he had left a brilliant career as a civil engineer to follow a quirk in his nature to join the RCMP. Thank heaven, the solicitor general thought, for that quirk, for Benson had risen rapidly and now headed up the political security section of the RCMP.

"Jim, good of you to get here so quickly."

"Ma'am—you know Ken Benson, I think?"

"Yes, we met last year in Calgary," the tired eyes smiled.

"You have a good memory, ma'am."

The solicitor general scowled. She disliked flattery and was suspicious of those who dispensed it. "Yes—well, sit down gentlemen; let's get down to business. Do either of you have any ideas?"

McUlroy spoke, the Scots accent barely discernible beneath the soft eastern drawl. "We have a profile of this man, but it's very sketchy. Victoria RCMP are working flat out to fill in the details and will fax an update shortly." He paused and pulled a file from his briefcase. While he was searching for his glasses, the solicitor general turned to Benson.

"What about the newsman, what's his name?"

"Kent, Paul Kent."

"Yes, Kent. I gather he went up to the man's hotel room and found the demands in an envelope. Is he implicated in any way?"

"No, he was evidently the last newsman to leave the room, and Mornay—that's the hijacker—told him where to find the envelope. He even gave Kent the key to his room. We've had him interrogated and it was apparently just by chance that he was chosen."

The solicitor general snorted. "I suppose it was just chance that he happens to work for the most vociferous anti-government paper in Canada and had the news spread world wide before we even knew about it."

McUlroy looked up, the half-moon glasses giving him the look of a quizzical owl. "There were nine other reporters in the room, ma'am. It's hardly reasonable to expect to keep such a story under wraps for even a very short time."

"Damn it, Jim, I know that! It irks me all the same." She exhaled noisily. "Well, go on. Let's hear all the bad news."

"The man's name is David Mornay and, yes, he is related to Nigel Mornay." He watched the solicitor general's eyebrows rise but, before she could speak, McUlroy continued. "He's the older brother who left home while still a teenager, joined the American Marines and served in Vietnam. After the war he took a degree in civil engineering and, until his early retirement, worked offshore. His wife was killed three weeks ago in a car accident and, according to initial information, he's taken it badly but seemed to be on the mend when the aircraft was hijacked."

"Why was he not with his daughter? Surely a six-year-old is a bit young to be travelling a long distance like that?"

"Mornay's father-in-law lives in South Africa and had a heart attack when told of his daughter's death. Mornay booked himself and the granddaughter on the hijacked flight but cancelled several days earlier and substituted his nephew to chaperon the child."

"Good reasons?"

"The story we get is that after his wife's death he was pretty run down and was persuaded to have a full physical examination. A piece of shrapnel was discovered in his neck right alongside the carotid artery. The metal is in a life-threatening position, and flying is out of the question until it can be removed."

"Shrapnel?" The solicitor general looked up from the pad she'd been doodling on. "How badly was he wounded? I presume this was in Vietnam?"

"Yes, and apparently he was wounded more than once. The Americans are not as forthcoming with information on his military background as they usually would be. It could be my imagination, but there seems to be a reticence to give us full disclosure. Nigel Mornay and Mornay's friend, a Chilean businessman, have been very helpful. They are desperately worried that the strain of the last few weeks and now the hijacking have pushed him over the edge."

"Is he capable of carrying out his threat? Did they give any indication as to his mental state?"

"Well, ma'am," this from Benson, "based on his profile, we have run a series of situation analyses through the computer and, unfortunately, the answer we get is that he is capable of carrying out his threat."

The solicitor general turned to McUlroy. "What's your feeling Jim?"

"The Chilean, Modesto, has known Mornay a long time and thinks it's quite a strong possibility. He feels that only the safe return of Mornay's daughter and nephew will keep the delegates alive." McUlroy removed his glasses and wiped the lenses on a clean handkerchief he pulled from his pocket. "As to his state of mind, who can say? According to Nigel Mornay, his brother has always been a reserved, self-contained individual, not a person given to irrational behaviour." He sighed, leaning back in the chair and clasping his hands behind his head. "This is a man accustomed to violence. His service record shows him to be a brave man. He has held senior positions in a tough industry, so obviously he has ability. The short answer is—I don't know, but I have a sinking feeling that this is a very dangerous individual and we'll have to tread carefully."

"I see. So how do you intend to handle this?"

McUlroy had expected the question. Politicians never picked up a hot potato if they could pass the problem along to someone else. He grimaced, the distaste fleeting on his face. "We have taken over from the local police forces and the hotel is surrounded, with all the guests removed. The Seattle police are sending us their top negotiator who was very successful in ending the militia hostage situation in March. Initially, we are going to try to talk him out."

"Is there no chance of rushing him with a tactical team? Get this over quickly?"

"None at all. He's in an upstairs suite. The only access is down a narrow passage, and he would have plenty of time to activate the bomb."

"What if he's bluffing? How can we be sure he has a bomb?" The solicitor general wiped her face, a memory of the failed Waco raid and her American counterpart on the hot seat loomed large in her mind. The room seemed suddenly warmer.

McUlroy shook his head. "I doubt that it's a bluff. His letter that Kent published itemises the chemicals he purchased. We've checked, and every single ingredient checks out. His Army record shows that he was trained in demolition work so I'd hate to risk a frontal assault on the assumption he was bluffing."

The solicitor general stood, leaning forward with both hands on her desk. "The political heat, as you can imagine, is intense. The PM is getting flak from all the Arab countries plus the UN. They are demanding a quick end to the situation, but" she looked at them sourly, "the delegates are not to be harmed—under any circumstances. You see, gentlemen, a solution to the Palestinian problem is imminent, and it looks like these hostages, some of them at least, will be the new leaders of a unified Palestinian state."

Ken Benson interrupted. "Surely ma'am, what about the Arab States persuading the hijackers to release the South African plane?

If that happens, Mornay would have no cause to hold the delegates."

The solicitor general controlled herself with difficulty. "Yes, Ken, that's the simple solution. Firstly, can you imagine any government admitting that it has links to organised terrorism? Also, the Arabs are worse than Orientals when it comes to losing face. What they want is the Israelis to release all their Hamas prisoners and for us to get their delegates out safely. But, yes, that is one of the options we are pursuing; however, we don't expect much help in that direction." She turned to face the window that overlooked the grounds on Parliament Hill. "The PM wants everything done to get the hostages out safely. He has given this case top priority, and you have full authority to make use of all federal government facilities, including the armed forces." She turned back to face them, and McUlroy felt a flash of sympathy at the lines of tiredness cutting into the slack face. "Your travel arrangements have been made. A military jet is waiting to get you to Victoria, so all I can do is wish you good luck. If you want to call your families, my secretary will place the call."

McUlroy shook his head. "No, ma'am, the sooner we leave, the sooner we'll get there." He stood up, a neat figure in his dark suit: "We'll do what we can."

"Yes, Jim, I know you will," she stuck out her hand. "It's terribly important that none of the delegates is harmed. There is more riding on this than I can tell you. I'm sorry to belabour the point; you know your job, but be extra cautious."

McUlroy felt suddenly irritated by the continual stress on caution and was about to retort when Ken Benson cut in smoothly: "Thank you, ma'am; we appreciate your confidence." He took McUlroy's elbow firmly, and the two made their exit.

Outside, McUlroy shook himself loose and growled, "What was all that about, laddie?"

"I heard a rumour just before we went in. The PM is getting egg all over his face about slack security and the solicitor general had to be very persuasive to get you and me put in charge of this."

"Oh did she now—and who did the PM have in mind—Jackson of Fisheries?"

Benson chuckled. "Wouldn't that be something, no—Pryor of Defence."

"Army!" He was incredulous. "My God, they are in a panic!" He looked at Benson, his face sombre. "Well, let's get a move on. If it's as big as she hinted, speed is all important."

A uniformed RCMP officer opened the door of the police cruiser and the two men entered. The door clicked shut, and the driver, a specialist in high-speed driving, pulled smoothly away from the curb, the flashers and siren coming on as he accelerated towards Ottawa's McDonald-Cartier International Airport.

Day 2:   1600 hrs.

Empress Hotel - Victoria.

Inspector Robert Nichols finished speaking to Ottawa and wearily replaced the receiver. It had been a long night. Sitting in his mobile command post on the lawn of the Empress Hotel, he wished desperately that the hostage expert from the Seattle PD would arrive soon. This whole situation was out of his province. His men, checking up on David Mornay's movements since the hijacking began, had confirmed his worst fears. Mornay had purchased all the ingredients needed to manufacture a bomb and the profile supplied by Ottawa proved that he had the expertise to build one. Nichols turned to his assistant. "Doug, those sharp shooters, have they arrived?"

"Yes, sir, they're assembled behind the Wax Museum in the ferry car park."

"Right! I want them deployed, just in case we get a clear shot at this madman." He drew circles on a map of the Inner Harbour and surrounding buildings. "Have two on top of the Provincial Museum and the Carillon Tower. Put another one on top of the Wax Museum."

"What about the Parliament Building? It's a good 200 metres away, but that might help."

"Yes, put two men up there, but make sure that the best shooter goes on the Carillon Tower. He'll have the best chance if the guy shows himself." He looked up sharply as a helicopter approached noisily across the Inner Harbour. "Get that bloody thing clear of this area," he yelled at the officer on the communications set. "Haven't Air Traffic Control issued a restricted notice over all of downtown?"

The young mountie on communications was already barking orders into his face microphone. A second later he switched on the overhead amplifier and Air Traffic Control came in loud and clear. . . . "Roger that, Firedancer; restriction on traffic over downtown has been in force for one hour." There was a brief pause then, "Helicopter, Golf Tango Victor, this is Victoria tower."

"Golf Tango Victor."

"Golf Tango Victor, you are in a restricted area, return to the airfield. I repeat—clear the area immediately."

"Tower, I have CTV news cameras aboard; request permission for one pass."

"Request denied: clear the area immediately."

The brightly painted helicopter clattered closer, obviously trying to get some film before being forced to turn. Nichols pointed to the hand microphone. "Override the tower and put me through to the pilot." The mountie switched channels rapidly.

"Golf Tango Victor, this is Firedancer. If you approach any closer, you and the CTV crew will be spending time in jail—clear the area NOW!" The last word snapped like the crack of a whip.

The helicopter jerked as if hit, the CTV camera crews cursing as they grabbed for handholds. The pilot heeled the chopper over in a tight arc, clattering back to the Upper Harbour and Selkirk Water.

Nichols wiped his suddenly sweaty palms on a rag lying on the table. His eyebrow twitched. "God damn, Mornay's letter specifically stated no helicopters whatsoever. Get Mornay on the phone and let's try to keep him calm." Nichols held the phone close to his ear while the communications man started the tape.

"Mr. Mornay, yes, I know . . .yes . . . yes . . . yes, I know what your instructions were, but that was a rogue flight by some bloody newsmen. We have cleared the area, and it will not happen again." A long pause then, "Yes, I will arrange that." He replaced the receiver and spoke to no one in particular. "He will shoot one of the hostages if another aircraft approaches and he wants a direct connect on this phone at all times."

"Direct connection?" queried Doug James.

"Yes, it's a simple hookup. If he picks up the phone he can

speak to us without going through the usual dialling procedure, and no one else can call him except through us."

"I wonder what he's up to?" mused James.

"It's a smart move. He wants his hands free. Will you arrange with BC Tel, Doug?"

"Yes, I'll set it up right away."

Nigel Mornay lifted the coffee cup before replying, took a sip, then carefully placed the cup on the table and looked up at the police psychologist. "I understand your position, Ross, but this is my brother we're discussing."

Rafa Modesto stood with his back to them, looking out of the window to the lawns that stretched down to the still waters of a small pond. He turned and snapped angrily, "For God's sake, man, don't you think we've tried to get to him. His letter specifically instructed the police to deny us any communication." He shook his head in frustration. "Nigel managed to get his phone number through contacts in the Empress Hotel, but as soon as he heard my voice he hung up. I tried again just ten minutes ago, but he's had some form of electronic block put on the line. Look, David is not some fanatic with a mission to change the world. He's a good man who has just lost the woman he loved, and now his daughter is in great danger, to say nothing of his nephew. Right now he is running on pure rage, and all we can do is wait for it to subside a little."

The psychologist pulled on his neatly trimmed Van Dyke beard that was flecked with grey hairs, and nodded reflectively. "Surely, then, if he is all you've told me, he'll not kill innocent people. This threat must be a bluff—granted a dangerous bluff, but a bluff nonetheless."

"You haven't been listening, Ross." Nigel Mornay held up a restraining hand to Rafa who was on the point of exploding. "David left home at 16 to join the marines—that alone should give you some idea as to his strength of will. He did three, not one, but three tours in Vietnam. When he came home after the war, he refused to kowtow to our father and left home without a penny. Then he managed by sheer hard work to rise through the ranks to a senior position in the mining industry. Don't you understand? He's more than capable of carrying out his threat, given the strain he's been under."

The psychologist, who had spent his life working with the criminally insane in Canada's prisons, sighed. He regretted the mild deception he had practised on these two men but he needed rock solid confirmation of his own earlier quick diagnosis. Picking up his slimline briefcase, he stuck out his hand. "Mr. Mornay, thank you for being so frank. I'm afraid that, despite what I've led you to believe, I happen to agree with your assessment, and my report will reflect that fact." He nodded to Rafa. "Mr. Modesto, please stay in touch with Inspector Nichols. We may yet convince David to talk to you."

Out of sight of the curious throng milling about behind the barricades along Government Street, six sharpshooters of the RCMP Emergency Response Team stood in loose formation, listening to a thin, neatly dressed man who used his hands a lot. Identically dressed in shapeless black nylon coveralls tucked into dark green jungle boots, each man wore a black woolen watchcap and carried a custom-made Winchester sniper rifle. These weapons were specially adapted for their role, being fitted with a lightweight stock and a Leopold 10x scope. Any of the six could hit a 50 mm circle at 150 metres. They had been trained to shoot from any position and at moving targets from stationary positions. They were no different from other RCMP officers, with the single exception that they were gifted marksmen and had been singled out for special training. This privilege meant that, in addition to their normal duties, they were required to practise a minimum of five hours target shooting each week. For this they received no extra remuneration beyond the personal satisfaction of knowing they were among the top marksmen in the Canadian police community.

Alvin Knight, at twenty-seven, was the youngest and the best, if such a word applied to men whose individual scores differed by fractions of a point. Knight stood with his head turned slightly, listening intently as Sergeant Drummond finished his briefing.

"Now remember, you are not, repeat not to fire until authorised to do so. We still don't know if the bomb will go off if he falls. We are all on line, so if you see a clear shot, call and advise Firedancer; he will authorise a shot or not as the situation dictates." As their instructor, Drummond knew their abilities and, without pausing, continued. "Knight, you will get up the Carillon Tower. It's the closest point and, although the angle is acute, you may have the best chance."

Knight nodded. He appeared outwardly calm, but his heartbeat increased and he felt a sudden hollowness beneath his ribs. "Yes, Sergeant."

Drummond ordered the others to various high positions on the Government and other buildings. Quickly, he checked their equipment. "Right! Make your way discreetly to your positions. Try not to be seen." He canvassed them briefly as they moved out. "Good luck."

Knight climbed inside the plain panel van with the others. The van moved south on Menzies Street, passing the Parliament Buildings, then turned east on Superior Street, finally turning north on Government Street. It was staying hidden from both the room which David Mornay occupied and the curious sightseers on Bellville and Wharf streets. Between the Parliament Buildings and the Provincial Museum, the driver stopped under the shadow of a giant oak tree. The men disembarked quickly, two disappearing into the Parliament Buildings and two into the museum.

Camouflaged in a large plastic raincoat, Knight walked to the base of the Carillon Tower. The iron gate was unlocked, and he climbed up the spiral staircase carefully holding the rifle close to his body to prevent damage in the tower's narrow confines. He climbed past the bells and scrambled up onto the roof where he lay flat behind the low concrete parapet that effectively hid him from view. He shrugged off the raincoat and placed the rifle on top of the folded plastic. Taking a small pair of high-powered binoculars from a pocket in his overalls, he methodically swept the facade of the hotel until he located the room holding the hostages. He noted that the curtains were drawn tight, but that one window was slightly open, and through the gap between the curtain and wall could glimpse a small section of the room that was perhaps 18 inches wide. He coughed and spoke into the boom microphone clipped to the headband over his watchcap.

"Firedancer, come in please."

Nichols replied at once. "Go ahead, this is Nichols."

"Knight, sir, in position on top of the tower."

"Right, Knight, you have your instructions. How good is your view up there?"

"Fine, sir, I can see through a small gap into the room, but it's a tiny area and appears unoccupied. The lights are on in the room."

"OK, Knight, keep a close watch. Check back to me every 15 minutes."

"Yes, sir." He pulled two pieces of chewing gum from a shoulder pocket and, without taking his eyes away from the binoculars, used his thumb to remove the silver paper before doubling the strips over and putting them into his mouth. The sun was behind him and, even if David Mornay had been aware of his presence, Knight would have been very difficult to see.

Chapter 13

Lisbon - Portugal

The Colonel's combat camouflage uniform was immaculate and his short haircut gave his scarred face an oddly boyish look. Balancing his weight on the balls of his feet, he pointed with a polished swagger stick to a huge blowup of the Cape Verde Islands on the committee room wall.

"The aircraft carrier, Principe de Asturias, is here," he stabbed the map. "By 1800 hrs today it will be 300 kilometres from Sal. The assault group will be lifted in 10 Sea King helicopters to Espargos. The helicopters will fly just above the sea to avoid radar and will deposit the assault group out of sight of the airfield here." Again the map dimpled. "We will split into two groups: group A will move close to the main terminal and control tower, while group B will position for the assault on the aircraft."

"What if you are seen, Colonel?" This from the minister of transport, his eyes red from lack of sleep. "What do you intend to do then?"

"There is always risk, but it will be dark. The weather forecast is for cloud cover down to two hundred metres in light rain. All the men chosen are expert in the techniques of silent attack—we have spent considerable time training with the SAS and the American Rangers on NATO exchanges."

"That does not answer the question, Colonel."

"I know that, sir. If we are seen, we will attack immediately and try to minimise casualties." Before the minister could interject, he continued: "There have been many successful operations and, as the minister is aware, only last month Dutch Special Forces released the passengers of that Surinam flight in Amsterdam. There is no reason why we should not succeed."

The Colonel's uniform was bare of decorations save the ribbon of the Order of Tower and Sword, Portugal's highest decoration for valour, and he bent the swagger stick in a small arc between his hands. No one in the smoke-filled room was ignorant of the

Colonel's service record in Angola and Mozambique and he was one of the very few officers who had refused to become involved in Spinola's coup against Caetano. Twenty years before, only the fierce loyalty of his para-commandos and the judicious shuffling of orders by well-placed friends in HQ had kept him and his men out of the surging revolution in the armed forces. With Spinola gone and a democratic system in place once more, a soldier who could not be swayed by politics was very valuable. A man whose integrity was absolute and whose skills in the dubious art of war were unquestioned was the automatic choice to lead the assault team.

He reached down and opened a plain wooden box at his feet and drew out what looked like a Medieval crossbow, but it was as far removed from the ancient crossbow as a musket was from a modern automatic rifle. Painted a flat black that seemed to absorb light, it looked deadly and evil. The bow was made of laminated glass fibre and carbon threads, while the body and stock were of ultra-light steel and aluminium. The cord running through an ingenious series of pulleys was of braided kevlar threads, giving a cross-sectional diameter of only three millimetres. He held it up in his left hand where it glinted like a grotesque surgical instrument. In his right hand he displayed a steel arrow, four inches in length, which looked like a silver ballpoint pen.

"This version of the modern crossbow, developed for sportsmen and hunters, has been improved by the Americans for precisely the kind of situation we are now facing. This arrow can penetrate six centimetres of hard wood at 100 metres. The stem is hollow and partially filled with mercury; it behaves on impact much the same way as a dum-dum fired from a conventional weapon." He glanced round the ring of silent faces. "A man hit in the head will drop without a sound. Ten soldiers split between the two assault groups have been trained in its use. Our plan is that group B with their archers will crawl to the edge of the apron lights and, at exactly 2055 hrs, execute the guards on the aircraft ramp and apron. We are relying on the silence of our attack to give us time to have men up the ramp and into the aircraft before the hijackers realise what is happening. Simultaneously the terminal and control tower will be attacked, and we expect to be in control by 2058 hrs.

"Tell me, Colonel," this from the minister of labour, "how did the hijackers gain control of the Espargos airfield in the first place?"

"Our intelligence indicates that two groups were involved. One group boarded in Vancouver or New York and this group commandeered the aircraft. The second group landed from the sea several hours earlier and established control of the airfield prior to the arrival of the SAA flight."

"It would indicate, Colonel, would it not, that this is a highly organised operation and must have taken considerable logistical support to put men ashore on Ilha do Sal to capture the airfield at the right time."

"That is correct, minister."

"Why then, Colonel, do you think they wanted the control tower and the terminal as well as the aircraft?"

"Get to the point, Mendes." The prime minister was not noted for his patience.

"I suggest, prime minister, that the hijackers realised, from previous unsuccessful hijackings, that an airfield is only a safe haven if they also control the tower and can use the radar as security to warn them of approaching aircraft or, for that matter, ships at sea."

"Colonel?" The prime minister sat at the head of the oval table, his hand cupped under his chin, the fat eyelids drooping.

"Minister Mendes is correct in his assumption. We have studied all the possibilities and his concern was one of them. However, the radar at Espargos cannot pick up targets moving slower than one hundred knots. Originally this was set to eliminate ground clutter and we will approach the island below that speed. At the same time as we are approaching the island, the Principe de Asturias will launch Harrier aircraft on a tangent to Sal to draw attention away from our approach."

Mendes remained dubious. "I still feel that the hijackers will have also considered these possibilities and, expecting us to launch a raid to rescue the passengers, will have taken steps to frustrate our efforts."

The Colonel showed a touch of impatience. "You would suggest then, minister?"

"That we let the Israelis and South Africans worry about it. If you fail, and passengers are killed we will be accused of bungling. If we succeed certain Arab States with whom we have invested much time in improving trade might be unhappy. Either way we lose."

The Prime Minister smiled wearily. "Anyone else wish to comment?"

A murmur ran around the table, and the chief of defence staff rose from his chair. His voice was even, but the knuckles of his fists were white from the pressure exerted on them as he leaned forward over the table.

"Prime minister, we have an obligation to the government of Cape Verde, and they have requested our help. It is also worth noting that the Americans have made a direct approach to us as they have no assets in the vicinity." He paused, as if to continue, then shook his head and sat down.

The minister of transport snapped angrily: "This is no time for heroics. We must . . ." He stopped short for the prime minister's hand was raised in the old imperial signal for attention.

"Thank you, Mendes. Half an hour ago I received a communique from the South African government." He now had their undivided attention. "They request permission to fly troops to Sal for a rescue attempt." He paused and stared sombrely at the group. "You realise the repercussions if we accede to this request: to have the problem solved by the South Africans, when we have an agreement with the Government of Cape Verde, would make us the laughing stock of the West. Portugal is not some banana republic and our companions in NATO will take a long hard look at us. No, we cannot pass this problem on to anyone else." He took a sip of water. "I have also received a message from NATO HQ South that the attackers of Espargos must have been landed by submarine as satellite surveillance can find no surface shipping close enough to Sal to have put men ashore. Our allies are desperately anxious to find which country is responsible. They want us to capture some of the hijackers for questioning."

"And what of the passengers?" This from the minister of tourism. "Do they not care if some, perhaps a great many, are killed?"

"Please, Paulo, let me finish! We already have two crew murdered. On the one hand, we have the South Africans who are determined to rescue their people and, on the other, we have NATO who wish to capture the hijackers alive in order to extract information. The assumption that we must have others rectify our problem is intolerable, and that is why I ordered the Colonel to have his men flown to the aircraft carrier Principe de Asturias which the Spanish government has placed at our disposal. I believe the Colonel's plan has a good chance of success; however, may I have a show of hands on this. All who agree to the plan as outlined, raise your hands." For a moment the room was silent, then all but the minister of transport raised their hands.

"Thank you." The prime minister turned to the Colonel. "You will join your men on the Principe de Asturias, Colonel. I understand that an aircraft is standing by." He searched for the right words, then lifted his shoulders helplessly: "May God go with you."

The Colonel snapped to attention, saluted, then turned and strode quickly out of the room.

―――――――――

The Colonel stood on the slowly rolling flight deck as the carrier butted its way south in a moderate swell and remembered the tense meeting of a few hours before. He scanned the skies again, searching for the anticipated arrival of the Harrier from Larbruch.

———————————

David Mornay took another turn around the hostages sitting or lying on the floor, testing their bonds carefully. He seemed indifferent to the pain some of them were in. Mike Monroe, his voice controlled and outwardly calm, had twice requested that David loosen the bonds for even a short period.

"Look, Mr. Mornay, we may be here for quite some time, and if the circulation is cut off for a long time a man could lose his hands."

David returned to sit on a table pushed up against the end wall, his legs dangling and his back resting against the embossed wallpaper. "Monroe, when the Viets captured men of my unit at Bac Tro they made them walk for three days with their hands tied behind their backs. It rained incessantly and was bitterly cold in the highlands." He rubbed his cheek with the barrel of the Walther. "Here you are in an air-conditioned room, no rain, no mud, and you have been bound for less than eight hours. Do you really expect me to feel sympathy?"

Ali Al-Azhar murmured gently, "You were soldiers, these men are not. What Mike says is true, and when this is all over, you will have to answer for your treatment of us."

"Al-Azhar, you seem to be an intelligent man. Think carefully for a second. Do you think that I am concerned over any consequences to myself?"

The Sudanese diplomat stared steadily at David. "No, but it becomes a consideration if you succeed."

Mornay did not answer for a long time and seemed to have sunk deep within himself. When finally he spoke, his voice was infinitely sad. "I do not believe any more than Yassin over there that the hijackers will release their hostages until they realise I am in deadly earnest."

A cold chill settled over the room as his statement sank in.

Monroe cleared his throat and croaked, "What do you mean?"

"I mean that I may have to execute one or more of you to prove my determination." As he spoke, he was looking at the Russian, Kuchinsky, who had gone chalk white. Beads of sweat stood out on his face and he appeared on the verge of fainting. "I suggest, Kuchinsky, that you save your fear until later. The reply is not overdue yet."

Ali Khufra had not spoken. Now he spat on the off-white carpet. "You call me a butcher, Canada, but what are you?"

"Very perceptive, Khufra." David's voice was dry. "Full marks, except you forget that it was you and yours that cast the first stone. You can hardly complain if I retaliate in kind."

Khufra eyes glittered with hatred. "Then you had better kill me, for if I live you will not," he snarled.

David smiled. "As you wish Khufra, but not before you have served my purpose."

"Do you not care for your own life?" the Sudanese asked.

David did not answer. Instead he touched his ear into which a fine cord disappeared. One end of the cord was attached to a hearing-aid insert, the other end going to a small box in his shirt pocket. He walked past the bound delegates toward the entrance door, then listened carefully before pulling a large Danish lounging chair across the space in front of it. While the delegates watched silently, Mornay upended several chairs and piled them haphazardly as well. Satisfied, he walked to the telephone and lifted the receiver.

"Nichols, listen very carefully. I have booby trapped the door, should you be entertaining any thoughts of a fast break-in with stun grenades. Also, you can remove the micro camera you started installing in the wall. You have thirty seconds."

In the command post, a stunned Nichols stared at his deputy in amazement. "How did he know?" Then flipping the switch, he asked. "How do we know that the hostages are safe?" There was no answer. Mornay had replaced the telephone. Nichols snapped at his communications officer: "Quickly, man, call the team back from the corridor, and tell them to remove the camera as well." He wiped his hands carefully on a florid paisley handkerchief, annoyed to find he was trembling slightly. Damn it all to hell, he was a police officer, not a politician. Above his head in the hotel suite, Mornay was kneeling beside the Sudanese diplomat.

"Tell me, Al-Azhar, what interest would the Sudanese government have in this affair?"

"I don't understand what you're driving at, but my government is not involved. What possible purpose could we have?" Al-Azhar shook his head. "You look for culprits where there are none."

Mornay lifted his eyebrows: "And what of the political asylum Sudan has given scores of Islamic fundamentalists from Egypt? Do you deny that your government has encouraged subversion all over North Africa and is actively involved with Iran in terrorist activity?"

"You define subversion to suit yourself, Mornay. We have other definitions."

"I'm sure you have, Al-Azhar, but it's not important. I don't care to indulge in political dialogue with you," he smiled grimly. "Compared to the Viets, you are not out of kindergarten yet. I only want you to realise that I consider you to be as guilty as these men." He indicated Khufra and Yassin with a sweep of his hand. "And you will suffer accordingly if my daughter or nephew is harmed."

"Do you honestly believe I have any influence over the hijackers? If so, you are sadly mistaken, and threatening me will not do any good."

"I think you do yourself an injustice, Al-Azhar. I doubt if your government will take kindly to a high-ranking diplomat being killed on Canadian soil as a direct result of lax security." He pointed at Monroe. "And the Canadian government will not want the worldwide embarrassment of such an event. On that you can bet your life," he grinned but without warmth, "no pun intended, but in fact that is what you are doing, all of you."

At the moment David Mornay was discussing the Sudanese

government's reaction to Al-Azhar's abduction, the Russian foreign minister was viciously castigating the Canadian government in a nationwide television broadcast. The broadcast was relayed to West European stations in time for the evening news and surprised many listeners with its harsh language. In Ottawa, the Sudanese Ambassador delivered a more restrained yet, in diplomatic language, 'strongly worded' note, requesting that all measures be taken to safeguard the hostages held in Victoria.

The strongest protest had been expected from the PLO. The PLO, surprisingly, confined itself to contacting the Canadian External Affairs Ministry with a request that it be kept fully informed. In the PLO offices in Gaza, the High Command had been in emergency session since the first news of the hostage taking. President Arafat and his cabinet were fully aware of the risks involved. He'd ordered his fledgling army to full alert and had quietly made sure that certain Hamas activists in the West Bank and Gaza were picked up and placed in secret detention centres. Word of these actions was leaked through a double agent to the Israeli government who, in turn, had been preparing retaliatory strikes against selected Hamas sites in Lebanon, Syria and Sudan. The Israelis were under intense diplomatic pressure to accede to the hijacker's demands and release their Hamas prisoners. In Tel Aviv, the opposition saw a heaven-sent opportunity to force concessions from Western governments, but the more sober realised that releasing the prisoners would not only wreak havoc with army morale but put some of the most dangerous guerrillas back into circulation. Those who were against any form of a deal considered the 12 known Israeli citizens on the aircraft as expendable. Within the governing party, only the prime minister and his cabinet were aware that Mossad's top field-agent was on the hijacked aircraft and how important were the secrets that Eli Natan carried in his head. It was an agonizing time, and David Mornay's capture of the political leadership of the PLO and Hamas had changed the picture entirely. The Israeli government breathed a collective sigh of relief and gave a silent prayer that Mornay could pull it off.

It didn't take Mossad long to get full details of David Mornay's background, for their intelligence network was vastly more sophisticated than anything Canada had in place. A Mossad agent, posing as a member of the Canadian Government Security Intelligence Service, tracked Rafa Modesto to Nigel Mornay's house in Victoria.

"Mr. Modesto, Mr. Rafa Modesto?"

"Hold on. Rafa, it's for you." There were a jumble of muffled voices before Rafa took the phone.

"Yes? This is Rafa Modesto."

The agent noted that the voice was not heavily accented. His briefing had been hurried, and the only reference to Modesto was that he was David Mornay's closest friend and was South American. The agent having been activated in Seattle only three hours before, cursed the shortage of information that arrived through the secure fax line.

"Mr. Modesto, my name is Halloran and I am a field officer with CSIS. I'm on my way to Rockland Heights and should be there in five minutes. I would appreciate a chance to discuss the situation with you. Can I pick you up? We can talk away from all the news media besieging the house."

Rafa hesitated. "I have already spoken to the RCMP and have just finished speaking to Ross, the psychologist. What more do you need to know?"

Halloran, whose real name was Dobkins, smiled to himself. His orders were to assess as fully as possible David Mornay's mental state and staying power. "Yes, I know, sir; it was our idea to have Ross talk to you. But I need to make my own assessment. For reasons I'm sure you can understand, I would prefer to do this as discreetly as possible."

"Very well, I'll walk up through the garden to the back gate which opens onto Rockland Avenue. You can pick me up there."

Fifteen minutes later the car sat in the parking lot on Mount Tolmie. The two men looked out over the city spread below them. "Let me get this straight, sir;—you are sure that he will carry out his threat to kill the hostages?"

Rafa did not reply immediately. He stared out over the lovely city spread out below them. Across the Strait of Georgia to their left, the Olympic Mountains sparkled in the clear air. Turning to face the agent, he sighed: "Look, I don't know— who knows how anyone will react, given such a unique set of conditions?" He paused, and Halloran waited. It had been an incredible stroke of luck getting to Mornay's closest friend without arousing suspicion. Thank God people in this country were so law abiding that a set of fake credentials could be accepted so completely. "You know that he fought in Vietnam for the Americans."

"Yes, we were aware of that. Why should it make any difference?"

"Once in a while, when the Black Dog came, he would tell me a little of his time in Vietnam."

"The Black Dog?"

"Oh yes, you wouldn't know about that would you. It's an old mercenary term to describe what happens when bad memories surface. A form of severe depression, anger and, I suppose, despair." Rafa smiled at a young couple strolling past their windscreen hand-in-hand. "It disappeared after he met Kate— his wife who just died—and he told me that after Laura was born he had almost forgotten his war, he . . ."

"You think it has returned, that he may be psychotic?" Halloran had read enough on delayed stress to realise that what Modesto was saying would scare the wits out of any officer tasked to free the hostages.

Rafa continued as if Halloran had not interrupted: " . . . He said—it was after Kate's death and I had just arrived from Chile— he said, and these are his words — 'she gave me back my life and taught me to laugh again. I saw and did many terrible things, and she took away my memories.' It was not like him to talk like that and he seemed for a moment to have forgotten that I was standing there. Then he said—and remember, this is a man not given to displays of violence, 'If that drunk had not died in the crash I would have killed him myself.'"

"Did you believe him?"

"At that moment, yes. I think a few days later he would have been embarrassed to be reminded."

"I see." Halloran looked away. He had the proof Tel Aviv wanted.

Chapter 14

Empress Hotel – Victoria

Victor Kuchinsky closed his eyes and tried to will the pain away. It came in waves, squeezing his chest with an iron band. He tried to speak, but his lips were numb. The pain now extended past his shoulders down his arm to his fingers. He groaned and toppled over. Sitting next to the Russian, Mike Monroe saw him fall and yelled out, "Help Kuchinsky; he's in trouble! Quick, Mornay!" He jerked at his own bonds in frustration.

Ali Al-Azhar swivelled round and rapped out, "In his pocket, a packet of capsules; he has a bad heart."

Mornay was across the room in three strides, keeping the Walther poised while he searched the Russian's heaving body. Finding a small plastic bottle, he checked the label then pocketed the Walther. He prised the Russian's mouth open and forced in a tablet. Kuchinsky's back, which had formed an arch between his head and buttocks, slowly relaxed, and he began to breathe easier, but his face was covered in a sheen of sweat and his eyes were glazed. Clearly his condition was serious.

"Mornay, you must get him medical assistance; he is gravely ill." The words tumbled from Monroe. "At least untie him. He can do you no harm in his present condition."

David ignored him, but his face was troubled as he stared down at the unconscious Kuchinsky.

"Mornay, Mike is right! He needs treatment; he is not a strong man," Al-Azhar begged, his composure for the first time showing signs of stress.

David picked up the telephone slowly, his mind a jumble of confused thoughts though nothing showed on his face.

Nichols was smoking a cigarette outside the radio cabin when he heard a yell from within the battleship grey vehicle. "Sir, telephone! Mornay's on the line." He dropped his cigarette onto the damp grass and ran up the steps into the confines of the command centre.

"Nichols here."

"Send up a doctor immediately. He must come alone and, above all, do not try to use him to gain entry."

"What's happened? Who is sick?" Nichols gripped the phone, his fingers white. "I need more information, for God's sake, man," but the phone was dead in his hand. He rapped the cradle desperately. "Connect me again," he snapped at the communications technician but, after listening a second, the tech shook his head.

"No use. He's pulled the jack out."

"Damn him, damn him to hell!" Nichols smashed his palm down on the metal desk with a bang that made the technician jump. "Corporal, we have two doctors standing by. Please call them over here at once." As Nichols replaced the dead phone, two men entered the small cabin, filling it entirely. "Get the hell out of here," Nichols snarled savagely, unable to see against the backlight.

"That bad, is it Bob?" Benson asked, stepping aside to allow the corporal to squeeze past. Nichols' head rocked up, and as he tried to stand he knocked back the swivel chair. For one hilarious moment the scene was reminiscent of a clip from a silent movie. Benson put his hand on Nichol's shoulder. "Sit down, Bob; no need for ceremony. What's the latest news?"

"I'm sorry, sir, Mr. McUlroy—we did not expect you for another hour. I thought you were more of those damned media people."

"What's the latest on the hostages?" McUlroy asked a trifle testily.

"He's just asked for a doctor, sir, but gave no details. We don't know who is ill or what the doctor is supposed to treat."

"Did you hear any shooting?" McUlroy was frowning.

"No, sir."

"Silenced weapon perhaps?" Benson murmured

"No, sir, or at least all the information from the correspondents who were released indicates that there was no silencer on the pistol Mornay was holding."

"You have doctors available, inspector?"

"I was sending for them when you and Mr. Benson arrived, sir. They should be here any minute now."

"Can you get in touch with Mornay and find out what the trouble is?"

"I'm afraid not. He's disconnected the telephone." At that moment a doctor arrived. A man in his early 30's, he'd responded to the call for volunteer doctors with enthusiasm, having spent a lot of his free time working with the local Civil Defence/ Search and Rescue program. There are certain people who, growing up in a gentle part of the world, become fascinated by violence whether natural or man-made. He was one of those, but, until now, fate had conspired to keep him away from any but the most trivial of adventures.

The Corporal stayed outside the communication cabin, which was now crowded, and called up to the occupants, "Dr. Hewson, sir. Dr. Carlyle is unavailable. There is an emergency down at the Black Ball ferry."

Hewson stood awkwardly, uncomfortably aware of the hard scrutiny. McUlroy stuck out his hand. "Doctor, my name is McUlroy; this is Ken Benson and, of course, you know Inspector Nichols." Hewson shook hands with each in turn. The run across from the temporary office where he had been sitting with other members of the police force had left him slightly breathless. McUlroy wasted no time. "The man holding the hostages has asked for a doctor."

"What's happened? Has there been a shooting?"

Ken Benson answered: "No. We are assuming that one of the hostages is in some sort of trouble. It could be an asthma attack, heart, epileptic seizure or any one of a number of things. Your emergency kit covers most eventualities, I take it."

"Yes, we try to anticipate the most common problems."

"Right, doctor, we want you to go up to the room as soon as possible." He looked closely at the doctor's face. "You are not to attempt anything," he paused searching for the right word, "heroic. We intend to plant a miniature microphone in the handle of your kit. Your task, besides tending to whoever needs help, is to position the bag where it can pick up conversation. Try to engage Mornay in conversation; we need to assess his state of mind." He drew deeply on a fresh cigarette. "That is all, doctor. Do nothing to aggravate him. You've been taught the drill: just keep a low profile."

For the first time Hewson felt the gut-tightening emptiness of real fear; keeping his head down, he nodded. He had not expected the brusque businesslike way Benson was briefing him. "Yes, yes, of course."

Benson watched Hewson and the corporal return across the grass to the office where the doctor would be prepared for his trip. "Think he can cope?" he asked Nichols.

"Yes, sir, I'm sure he can. It's just 'Buck-fever.'"

"Hmm," McUlroy snorted; "this fellow, Mornay, still has the initiative, and until we can turn the flow around we're not going anywhere fast." He motioned to the technician. "Try getting him on the line again."

The mountie pushed a reset button and flipped up a toggle switch. They all waited expectantly. "It's ringing, sir." A sudden look of consternation crossed his face. "Oh, oh, he's pulled the jack again."

McUlroy spoke almost to himself. "We had better walk carefully with this one; he's determined to keep us off balance."

Nichols spoke into a separate microphone, "Despard. The doctor with you? Right, see that the bug is placed in the handle of the emergency kit. Place another somewhere on the doctor's outer clothing, . . .what? . . . I know he might find it, that's the general idea, he might not look any further and the one in the handle is hard to detect."

Benson nodded approvingly. "Good thinking, Bob. Still, it's a hell of a risk—what if Mornay shoots the doctor when he finds the decoy."

"I'm gambling that he wouldn't have called in a doctor without assuming that we might try to sneak in a bug. He could easily have let whoever was in trouble suffer, so the fact that he called in a doctor indicates that he is not quite as ruthless as he wants us to believe."

Chapter 15

Ilha do Sal: Espargos Airfield.

Ibram Khalil had seen it coming. The bulk of the hijackers were like himself—skilled guerrilla fighters who had been chosen for this mission mainly on their competence in battle. But this was another kind of war, and, despite the ease with which they had overrun the airfield, they were concerned by the total absence of cover. Having in the past been subjected to the attentions of the Israeli Air Force, they knew full well the dangers of being caught in the open. Earlier, Davis had advised them of the reason for the delay in the planned executions, and the stunning news of Mornay's coup had left them wondering what options the blond colonel and Kassim now had. Kassim had not improved the situation by his blustering threats to execute the passengers in blocks of ten.

A general discussion among the men became heated, and a scuffle ensued between two of the group: one of the guerrillas suggesting the plane with its load of passengers be flown to Beirut in Lebanon, while the other was determined to see the release of the political prisoners (his brother being one) before any deviation from the original plan. Davis had stopped the squabbling with a combination of quiet confidence and veiled threats. Khalil watched admiringly while Davis alternately praised their courage and lashed their lack of faith.

"Do you think," he concluded in fluent Arabic, "that the central committee has not already made plans for this situation. I tell you once again that the Zionists are under great pressure from many quarters to release our comrades in jail. Soon we will be on our way back home, but whatever happens you are soldiers, specially chosen. Do not fail the great cause for which we fight. The Central Committee will reward our efforts well, but they will also take note of those who for selfish personal reasons would jeopardise our mission." A chill had settled over the cabin, for all present had witnessed the committee's anger in the form of Ali Khufra and none wished to be on the receiving end of such cruelty. But the hours had dragged and the long night without news had not been easy on the nerves. Kassim had rotated the guards every hour and, more than once, a burst of fire into the dark night from a jittery sentry had raised tensions to fever pitch.

Most of the passengers were awake. All had passed a restless night, and the queues outside the washrooms were long. Earlier Davis allowed airport staff to replenish the Boeing's water and fuel tanks, but now water to flush the toilets was gone. Tempers among the passengers, frayed by uncertainty and tiredness, flared on more than one occasion. A hijacker watching the dispirited passengers was only half aware of a sharp exchange of words between two women outside the middle set of washrooms, between the smoking and non-smoking sections. One of the women suddenly slapped the other, the noise alerting the guard. He moved quickly across to investigate.

Khalil had just entered the main door to discuss perimeter security with Kassim when the scene unfolded. On reaching the women, the guard pushed the two struggling combatants apart. The larger of the two, an overweight woman with prominent breasts under a thin cotton T-shirt, brushed the guard's arm aside in an attempt to strike the other woman again. Incensed at this disdain for his authority, the guard slapped the woman hard across the face and, grabbing a handful of the woman's T-shirt, yanked her back and forth like a rag doll. The T-shirt ripped, and the woman fell heavily, her short skirt flaring above her waist. The stunned woman tried futilely to cover her naked breasts protruding through the torn T-shirt.

A burly South African whose own self-control had been under pressure ever since the landing on Sal, jumped up. A farmer, he ran his five thousand morgen property with an iron hand. His labourers were better cared for than most and his staff turnover was low, but, like most right-wing white South Africans, he still had difficulty coming to terms with the new reality in his country. To have dark-skinned hijackers dominate his country's aircraft was bad enough, but to strike a white woman was more than he could take. The quiet pleading of his tiny wife had until now kept him sullenly in his seat, but this ultimate insult could not be endured. The farmer rose with a roar, a huge arm snapped around the guard's neck, the other crushing the wrist that held the AK47. The guard sagged, struggling to get leverage as he was lifted off his feet.

Ibram Khalil sucked his breath in sharply and was already halfway down the aisle before the AK47 dropped from the guard's hand. The heavy .45 automatic in Khalil's hand swung in a short arc and smashed van Zyl behind the ear. The Afrikaner stumbled and began to turn, slackening his grip on the guard. Balancing on the balls of his feet Khalil swung again, the barrel of the automatic cutting into the thick flesh where the massive neck joined the shoulders.

Khalil remembered the Russian instructor saying years ago, "Hit here, not half an inch away, right here," the pain flaring as he demonstrated on Khalil's neck. Van Zyl dropped, his knees caving as the massive body fell between two seats before sliding to the floor, dragging the guard down with him. Now Khalil stood, feet flat, his nostrils flaring as he sucked air into his chest. The heavy automatic covered passengers, many half out of their seats: "Sit down all of you, sit down," his voice pitched high as the adrenalin rush began to subside. The guard disentangled himself from the unconscious van Zyl and stood, massaging his throat, eyes wild with rage. He kicked viciously at the body, then picked up his rifle and smashed the butt down on the upturned face.

"Back to your position," Khalil snarled, shoving the guard away. The guard hissed back: "It was planned, Khalil. We must shoot him, the women also."

Khalil's face glistened with a thin sheen of sweat. "Do as you're told," he growled, then added more softly, "they will be punished."

With a last kick into van Zyl's ribs, the guard reluctantly moved away, muttering oaths. Khalil watched him go and motioned the other guards back to their places.

In the cockpit, Davis listened on the co-pilot's headphones while Captain Strydom spoke to the tower. "Yes, I understand . . . He is listening in . . . right, standby!"

Instead, Davis removed his headset, and Strydom saw with alarm how angry he was. "So, now he tells us what to do, does he?" Davis seemed unaware of Strydom's presence, The silence was total; even the whine of the air-conditioning seemed hushed. "Until 6 pm Pacific Standard Time, what will that be here, Captain?" Strydom had mentally worked out the time difference as soon as the radio operator in the tower had relayed Mornay's conditions to the cockpit.

"It will be midnight here."

"I hope for all your sakes he is bluffing, Captain." He pushed the transmit button. "Tower, check with New York again. Tell them I expect a reply to our demands within the hour."

The tower controller, a dark-haired, stocky Portuguese from the Spanish frontier town of Vita Formo whose most notable characteristic was the short temperedness of its inhabitants: "Damn it, for the tenth time, the Israelis are not responding to any pressure from the UN or the Americans. The Americans insist they are doing everything they can."

Strydom thought for a second that Davis would explode. He interrupted quickly: "Let me talk to New York." Davis' thin lips compressed into a narrow line before he finally acquiesced. "Do it now," he whispered.

Strydom keyed his own microphone. "Tower, patch me direct to New York." He waited, then, "New York, this is Captain Strydom. Please advise all parties that the status here is deteriorating . . . what? . . . No, all executions are on hold until midnight, but the situation is changing quickly. Please understand we need a positive reply as soon as possible."

Davis nodded approvingly, colour returning to his face. "Very good, Captain; just as long as you keep up the pressure on them."

At that moment a buzzer sounded behind Strydom's head and he unclipped a small bulkhead mounted microphone. "Yes?"

Davis leaned forward and took the mike out of Strydom's hand as the overhead speaker crackled. "Comrade Colonel there is trouble in the main passenger compartment; come quickly."

With an oath, Davis rose to his feet and pushed past a guard. "Do nothing, especially don't use the radio." He barked orders to the guard standing behind the co-pilot's chair, yanked the curtain aside and strode out into the upper lounge.

Kassim was sitting in a seat facing Eli Natan and the other VIP prisoners. He was telling them in loud and broken English what he was going to do with them if the Israelis did not immediately release their Hamas prisoners. Colin listened fascinated and repulsed, his stomach heaving as Kassim described the procedure to be used on the Israeli captives. The dark face was animated and the eyes glittered. He pointed at Laura and was about to speak when Davis stormed into the lounge. "Kassim, come with me, there is trouble." He did not pause and was halfway down the staircase before the bemused Kassim had gathered his wits.

Davis reached the group clustered around van Zyl, with Kassim five paces behind. Mrs. van Zyl was on her knees, her husband's battered face in her lap. Khalil stood warily, the automatic pistol loose in his hand.

"What happened, Khalil?"

Without taking his eyes off the passengers sitting fearfully in their seats, Khalil gave Davis and Kassim the gist of the story. Kassim spoke first: "He must be shot. It will serve as a warning to the others." He put out his hand and roughly pushed Mrs. van Zyl back.

"Nie, nie, " she sobbed, holding her husband's head from which blood still flowed onto her print dress.

Kassim growled and pushed harder, then Davis spoke: "Wait! Our people are still held. If we kill this fool, one of ours may suffer." He squeezed Khalil's shoulder. "Well done, Ibram."

"Wait, wait, all you tell us to do is wait. Tell the Israelis to release our men or we blow up the plane and kill all the passengers." Kassim was beside himself with rage.

Davis stared at him, his eyes going flat. The moment seemed to last forever. "Right! Kassim, take him outside and shoot him," his breathing was shallow and his colourless eyes pierced Kassim; "but when the man in Canada kills one or more of his hostages in reprisal you will answer to the Committee."

"Why do you not tell this man in Canada that we will kill his daughter if he does not release our people."

Davis smiled mirthlessly. "Kassim, he was a soldier, a marine who fought in Vietnam. What do you know of such men? No, don't answer. If you knew, you would not speak as you do." He turned to Khalil. "Find if there is a doctor on the passenger list; ask the stewardess; have him attend this man." Glad to be doing something, Khalil grunted assent in Arabic and went off to find a stewardess.

"What makes you so sure that this man in Canada will not give in if we threaten his daughter?"

"Comrade Colonel," Davis said warningly,

"Comrade Colonel," it came reluctantly, but it came.

Davis stared at Kassim, his expression cold, but when he spoke his voice was patient, almost as if he were a schoolmaster and Kassim a particularly stupid pupil: "Because the marines this man fought with retook Hué, a town you probably have never heard of. In doing so, they broke the back of the North Vietnamese Army who were also very good soldiers. Understand, this is not a man who surrenders." He put an arm around Kassim's shoulders in a conspiratorial manner and drew him away from the passengers and other guards. "When I was in the People's Republic I was taken to their museum of American atrocities. I was shown and told things I have not forgotten; so, believe me, my friend, I cannot run the risk that he is bluffing."

Unappeased, his anger at the rebuke still evident, Kassim spoke: "And what, Comrade Colonel, do you intend to do if he does not release our leader?"

"He is one man, Kassim. He will tire and, when he does, he will make an error. We have men, the island and time. We will wait." He drew a deep breath and, before Kassim could speak, added, "We will wait until dawn tomorrow, then act." Davis looked searchingly at Kassim. "Comrade Major, you were chosen very carefully for this mission, as all were. I do not expect my orders to be disobeyed."

Kassim watched him go. He had never understood why the Russian had been chosen by the committee but had noticed how he was deferred to, and his own orders had been explicit: "You are to obey the orders of the Comrade Colonel without question, Kassim. Once you join forces on Ilha do Sal, he will be in complete charge. If he is killed, you will be in charge, and, if you die, Khalil will act in your place. However, be advised that his safety is very important to us." The grizzled grey head had peered up at him through half-moon glasses, then dismissed him with a nod.

Davis climbed back up the staircase to the upper lounge. He was so deep in thought that he reached the top stair and kept climbing. Encountering only air, he stumbled forward. He grabbed at the rail to support himself and missed the chrome-and-wood bannister. Doing a rapid shuffle to stay upright, he found his footing and looked up to see Colin Mornay's cool amused eyes on him. For a long moment the two men locked eyes before Colin looked away. Davis felt a shiver run through him, for this was a branch from the same tree, and he suddenly felt very old. He looked for Eli Natan and, finding the Israeli's face at the rear of the cabin, called to him, "Mr. Natan, please come with me." The look of stunned astonishment that quickly crossed the Israeli's face and was just as quickly erased was worth the whole trip, Davis thought dryly. "Yes, we know who you are. Come to the cockpit."

Eli Natan, like all of the other passengers with the exception of Colin, was unaware of the drama unfolding in Victoria. He rose to his feet, feeling the ashes of defeat harsh in his mouth.

Someone had penetrated their security in Washington. No wonder they had beaten him up when he was first pulled from his seat. Eli Natan was an exceptional man by any standard and now he knew why the hijack had occurred. Israel would have to bargain if they wanted him back. Davis stood aside and sardonically introduced him to Captain Strydom. Eli noticed the purpling bruise and gash on the Captain's head and wondered what had prompted it.

"Mr. Natan is going to broadcast. He will speak directly to the Israeli authorities."

The battered face showed no surprise, but appeared if anything to be slightly amused: "Really?" It was no more than a murmur, but the strength of will was evident.

"Yes, Mr. Natan, really. . . You are going to tell the Israeli government that, unless they comply with our demands by dawn, we will begin to execute passengers every hour after that time. You, of course, will not be shot immediately but subjected to . . . ah, interrogation. There are men out there who would very much like to question you."

Natan's face paled slightly, but his voice was steady: "I see. I think, however, that you place too high a value on my life. I am not, despite what you may have been told, essential to the Israeli government. They will not bend—you of all people should know that."

"You know me?" It was Davis' turn to be startled.

"Bullseye," Eli thought with grim satisfaction. "Only by reputation. You and Carlos are in everyone's files."

Davis rewarded Eli with a tight smile that did not reach his eyes. "You underestimate yourself, Natan, but that is why we will shoot passengers as well. Imagine how the world is going to react when we advise them that because of one Israeli agent a hundred or more innocents had to die."

Natan did not remove his eyes from Davis' face, but something puzzled him. Why had they not started with their program? The plane had been on the ground for over 15 hours and obviously he had been identified almost as soon as the plane landed. Why had they not forced him to call Israel at once. Perhaps they were trying to protect their agent in Washington. Something obviously had stayed their hand—but what? "And if I refuse?"

"Tell him, Captain, how we persuade people."

Captain Strydom turned in his seat, and Eli saw the suppressed rage behind flat eyes. "They will take another of my crew, probably one of the stewardesses, a young one you can be certain." He was about to continue then, with a shake of his head, turned back to stare out of the window. Davis picked up the headset and motioned Natan to sit in the co-pilot's seat. He put out a hand to help him to fit the headset, but was shrugged off. Davis snapped on the overhead speaker.

"OK, Captain, call the tower and have them patch us through to Tel Aviv." Earlier, technicians from the assault team had fitted their satellite communication system to the tower controller's set. This now allowed the cockpit to communicate with the tower, and the tower to communicate worldwide.

"Tower, this is Xray Lima;" the very routine nature of the call gave Strydom a lifeline in the present sea of insanity.

"Xray Lima, go." The Portuguese controller was startled.

"Tower, connect us directly to the Israeli Government in Tel Aviv."

"Roger, Captain, switching now . . . stand by . . . you are connected."

Eli Natan hesitated. For a professional spy this was the hardest thing he had ever been forced to do. He knew his career as a Mossad officer on overseas assignments was ended. If he survived this debacle, these men would make certain his description was circulated worldwide. Clearing his throat he began: "This is Eli Natan. Who is receiving, please?"

"Mr. Natan, my name is Avram Livinsky. I am with the Ministry of Foreign Affairs in Tel Aviv."

Eli's heart leapt. Avram was the secret acronym for Mossad's counter-terrorist unit. "Mr. Livinsky I have been instructed to advise you that the Hamas group intend to murder a group of passengers every hour after dawn." He knew what he had to say next but hated saying it all the same. "I am suspected of being an Israeli agent employed by Mossad and will be subjected to implemented interrogation at that time." Now they knew for sure that there was a mole in the Washington Embassy and that his cover had been blown wide open.

"Your message has been received and will be passed to the prime minister. Are you well?"

Davis cut the switch that controlled communications before Eli could answer. The question meant, of course, can you hold out? Eli sighed and removed the lightweight headset. "You will not succeed. You must know that."

"We have already achieved our main aims. All that remains is confirmation that our men are free from your jails, and that will come before morning." The rugged impassive face looked at Eli and, for a fleeting moment, the Israeli agent saw something behind the colourless eyes. What was this man afraid of? Trained by Mossad's top psychologists to assess and judge people from all walks of life, Eli knew that the man facing him was not quite as sanguine as he made out.

Davis motioned for him to leave the flight deck. Eli levered himself out of the seat and tiredly stretched his back muscles. As he pushed through the curtain, his gaze met that of the young man who had come upstairs earlier, and Eli noted that the young girl with him was awake and leafing through a flight magazine. He liked the cool level look the young man gave him and made a mental note to try and talk to him when the opportunity arose.

Chapter 16

Atlantic Ocean

Ten SH-3D Sea King helicopters clattered low over the grey Atlantic swell. Behind them and fast disappearing into the night, was the Spanish helicopter carrier, Principe de Asturias. Colonel da Silva sat behind the pilot in the lead helicopter, his map case and Magellan position locator open on his knees. For the tenth time he studied the map of Ilha do Sal, checking again the strategic points on the airfield. The men with him were the cream of Portugal's Armed Forces, each chosen by the scar-faced colonel personally.

In normal use, the giant helicopters were fitted with banks of electronic detection equipment monitored by two sonar operators trained in anti-submarine warfare techniques. To make way for da Silva's troops, all removable items were out, but there was much that could not be removed in time, and the ten men in each helicopter sat uncomfortably on improvised seating. The atmosphere within the cabin was extraordinarily cheerful. Noise from the turboshaft engines was deafening, yet bursts of laughter rose above the clattering of the blades. A casual observer might have been forgiven for thinking these men were on their way to a rest camp or leave period. In fact, for all of them, the chance to go on this operation was a heaven-sent opportunity to break the monotony of peace-time service, and had the little colonel sought volunteers, he could have doubled his contingent.

Five men in each of the two lead helicopters carried glass and steel crossbows, similar to the one displayed by the Colonel in the cabinet room. As the colonel had stated earlier, these much-improved versions of the medieval crossbow were capable of killing a man up to 100 metres away without making a sound. The Colonel sat mulling over the telephone call received prior to his being airlifted to the carrier.

"Colonel da Silva?"

"Speaking."

"Colonel, this is General Matson, NATO Group South."

"Yes, sir."

"Colonel, we require, as you know, at least one of the hijackers alive. Do you have a contingency plan?"

"Sir, my orders are to save the passengers but, of course, we will do what we can."

"Colonel, if my information is correct, you intend to use the RH weapon to neutralise the perimeter guards."

Da Silva marvelled at how fast news travelled in the rarefied atmosphere of high government and army circles. "That is correct, sir."

"Colonel, I want you to use the paralysing dart on at least two of the perimeter guards."

"We have only the instant-kill type, sir."

"So I understand. There is a Harrier on its way to you now with a supply of the paralysing type. The pilot has instructions to hand them to you personally."

"Sir, how fast does the drug work?"

"I am told, Colonel, it is almost instantaneous, but have your men aim high in the body. A Dr. Carmichael is also arriving with the Harrier. His job is to administer the antidote."

"General, if one of the guards cries out before the drug works, it could have disastrous results."

"I'm aware of the risks, Colonel, but our technical people tell me that its effect for all practical purposes is instantaneous. That's why Carmichael must administer the antidote very quickly or the target will suffocate."

"With respect, General, I cannot agree to use the paralysing dart on the perimeter guards. They must be silenced with absolute certainty. If only one manages to cry out, a lot of people will die."

"Colonel, your government has given you the green light to go ahead and deal with the terrorists as outlined in your plan, but within a few minutes your prime minister will be on the line. I suggest you do as he orders." There was a click, and da Silva was abruptly cut off.

As Matson had predicted, the phone rang again within five minutes, and the prime minister came on the line.

"Da Silva, it is very important that one of the hijackers be taken alive, but do nothing to endanger the passengers. NATO and the Americans are desperate for information on how the group came ashore at Sal. Do you understand?"

Yes, thought da Silva bitterly, I'll be damned if I do and damned if I don't. "It will be very difficult, but we will do our best, sir."

Now he sat musing, his original plan still in force but modified by the requirement to take at least one of the hijackers alive. Earlier, a Harrier Jump Jet had landed on the Principe de Asturias's flight deck, and a fat and talkative Dr. Carmichael had emerged, puffing with his 'bag of tricks' as he called it. The pilot handed da Silva a container the size of a bread box containing darts. These were identical to the killer barbs, except for a white band a half centimetre wide around the tip. The doctor explained sagely: "Pressure tip, Colonel. When it hits the body, an internal needle is driven deep into the flesh and a pressure valve is released, forcing the solution deep into the tissues."

"How long before the effect takes place, doctor?"

"It varies, of course, with the individual and the location of the strike."

The Colonel's scars were very evident and he rubbed his nose as if continual smoothing would remove the ridges that laced his face. People close to him would have recognised the signs of deep anger, yet his voice was controlled.

"The worst and best case situations, please."

"Well, we have not tested it fully, you understand; lack of targets . . . ha, ha . . . and volunteers . . . after one shot, don't wish for another . . . ha, ha."

"The results, doctor?"

"Rum fellow," the doctor would say later, "never blinked . . .

eyes went right through one . . . a very cold fish for a Pork Chop what . . . ha, ha." The merriment faded from the doctor's face and he cleared his throat. "The best, Colonel, is instantaneous: usually from a hit high in the upper body close to the head. The worst is about three seconds from a hit low on the thigh on a larger than average male."

"Then a man could call out before he lost consciousness, could he not, doctor?"

"Not in any of the tests we have carried out, colonel, not a peep, ha, ha."

"But you admit that the drug has not been thoroughly tested and the possibility exists?"

Rattled, the doctor stammered: "Well . . . anything is possible, but . . ."

"What about recovery? How long can a man lie before the antidote is administered?"

"Only about three minutes, Colonel, then the lungs collapse, asphyxiation occurs."

"Thank you, doctor," da Silva dismissed him curtly. Now he wrestled with the decision. If he ignored the request of NATO HQ and used the solid barbs to kill the perimeter guards, he would stand a far greater chance of saving the passengers, but his career would be cut short. Matson would see to that. If he used the drug darts, the chance of a guard crying out would be greatly increased. Finally, before climbing aboard the lead helicopter, he called Castella to one side. The giant mulatto sergeant nodded as da Silva outlined his plan.

"Use the solid darts with the exception of those on the gangway. You, Castella, will make it your responsibility to see to those two. Use the best archers we have and make certain they hit high."

Castella saluted. With more decorations than his much-decorated Colonel, he was a legend in his own right, but a penchant for wine and women had kept a commission out of reach. The briefing had been thorough; da Silva had made a point of passing all information on to his troops, no matter how irrelevant. Part of his success in the bush wars of Angola and Mozambique had been due to this policy. None of the hundred men tasked for the assault were in any doubt as to the political, military and logistical problems associated with the attack.

The Sikorskys skimmed over the sea, barely metres above the grey sullen swell. It was 4 a.m. on Ilha do Sal.

Chapter 17

Vancouver B.C.

In Vancouver ten men were being dragged from their beds. These were the best of the RCMP's and city police emergency response teams. Selected from the special units in their districts, all had received training in diplomatic hostage taking. Canada is not a land of violent passions, and the local police forces, in alliance with the RCMP, could and did handle all but the most exceptional cases, such as the FLQ scare in the 1970s' when the regular army was brought in. Spurred by the rising crime rate, the popular press, and a desire not to be outdone by the Americans, ERT teams were formed, and the best men drawn from these units were, in turn, trained intensively in specialised situations such as the one that now faced them.

Now they sat, quietly talking in the air-conditioned lounge at Vancouver International Airport, surrounded by the paraphernalia of their trade. Their commander began to brief them. "The man in Victoria still controls the situation. He is in a very strong position strategically but must be getting tired. We will attempt to take him before his deadline expires." A ring of silent faces watched him closely. "He is in *this* room," pointing to a plan faxed earlier, "and there is only one way in, through this door, so we must try to take him after breaking the door down. We will use a radio-activated mini charge to blow the door in and stun grenades to keep him off balance." He took a deep breath: "The only reason this has not been proposed earlier is that this man is known to be an expert with explosives. Our information indicates that he is wired in some way to an explosive, so killing him might activate a trigger when his body hits the floor." The commander looked at the faces before him and felt a gut-tightening uneasiness. This had the feel of a bad one. "Our best assessment of his psychological profile indicates that he will hesitate long enough for us to neutralise the threat. We cannot use firearms in such a small room, so I want some ideas—yes, Butch."

"A throwing knife, sir, in the throat; both hands will instinctively grab for it. We can hold him upright until he is searched."

"Hmm—messy, but it might work. Anyone else?" He scanned the faces looking at him, but no one spoke. He sighed: "OK, who is the best knife man? . . . Jeff . . . you will throw the knife, which means you must be first through the door. Now, all the delegates are bound and lying on the floor, and Mornay will be sitting or standing. He has something that warns him of approaching trouble; I'm told it's an electronic device that he picked up before the hostage taking. Jamming will commence five seconds before we move into the corridor, so speed is vital. Murray, you and Bert will attach the charges and blow the door. Jeff goes straight in with the knife. Butch, you and Arnie will throw stun grenades and grab Mornay before he falls."

"What about entry through the window, sir?"

Yes, I'm coming to that. There are heavy drapes across the windows, and the windows are the old-fashioned, heavy type which will have to be blown as well. Cliff, you and Johal will be lowered from the roof with another radio-activated mini charge set to the frequency that Murray will have. When Murray blows the door, the window will go at the same time. Timing is vital, so I want this all over in ten seconds from the time the door goes down." He looked at the men who trusted his judgement and again felt a shiver run through him. "The strategy can change if other information becomes available, but this is the best we can come up with for the moment. On arrival we will review the situation; for the time being, study that layout until you know everything about it."

Outside, a fan-jet Falcon of the RCAF was moving into position ready to load the ERT team, the whine of its jets inaudible to the men in the lounge.

In Moscow, the Hamas man and the ex-chief of the KGB were in deep conversation. On the table lay the latest satellite photographs of Ilha do Sal. The ex-chief still had influence where it mattered, and getting classified photographs was the easiest part of his planning. The photographs showed the island and a 400-kilometre stretch of sea east of the island.

As Doctor Hewson walked along the thickly carpeted corridor, his hands were clammy with sweat. The emergency case in his right hand seemed to weigh a ton and he desperately wished the electronics man had made a better job of taping the button microphone into the handle, for it felt like an acorn under his hand.. Now that he was playing out one of his fantasies, he felt nothing but a hollow fluttering fear in the pit of his stomach. He cursed, trying to control his shaking with deep slow breathing. The policemen guarding the corridor had murmured, "Good luck, doc," and, until that moment, he'd nearly convinced himself that he could turn back and refuse the assignment. Now his fear of ridicule conquered his fear of dying and the mounties' thumbs up and grin evaporated the last of his resolve to retreat.

The door loomed large in front of him. Hewson put the metal case down and rapped on the door, forgetting to step to one side as instructed by the mountie sergeant: "Just a precaution, doctor—it doesn't pay to take chances." Silence, cold total silence. Perspiration ran from his armpits and the smell of his own fear was rank in his nostrils. He raised his hand to knock again, when a voice called softly: "Enter very slowly—very, very slowly."

Hewson turned the doorknob and the door swung on oiled hinges. He pushed the door open slowly, forgetting for an instant the case at his feet and, as he stepped past the door, his foot caught the case and he stumbled into the room. A big, solid, hard-looking man sat in a chair in the middle of the room, a pistol in one hand pointed squarely at Hewson's mid-section while the other rested on a bag in his lap. Hewson tried to explain: "I'm sorry, the case . . . I fell . . ."

"Calm down, doctor. Bring the case inside, and lock the door." The accent puzzled the doctor as it was strange but not quite foreign. Hewson could detect traces of Australian or South African, and, although the Canadian accent was slight, it was still there.

Until the man spoke, Dr. Hewson had been totally unaware of the bound figures lying and sitting on the floor. His eyes opened wide in astonishment and, although briefed on what to expect, the reality was startling, and the bizarre scene held his attention. "What?"

"I said, doctor, bring your case inside and lock the door."

"Yes, of course." Hewson complied and, now that he was in the room, his fear began to subside. He snapped the case open and placed it on an ornate coffee table between two chairs.

"Step away from the case, doctor."

"For heaven's sake, it's a standard medical emergency case," he replied, startled.

"Doctor, I think it's time you learned the rules. At all times you will do exactly as I say." He raised a hand. "Please understand the stakes are high and, while I wish you personally no harm, any foolishness on your part could cause the death of everyone in this room. Yours as well."

Hewson, staring at the cold grey eyes, tried to hold them and failed. He recalled something from his childhood: his father speaking of a neighbour, a retired, weather-beaten Saskatchewan farmer who had subdued two thugs attempting to burgle his home. "Some men you never push. Size has nothing to do with it. Some men, very few unfortunately, like the wolverine, are afraid of nothing. They'll keep coming at you no matter what the odds are, until they win or die trying."

"Come over here doctor, and turn around."

Hewson felt Mornay's hand checking for weapons. A hand went into his jacket pocket, first the left then the right: "Take your jacket off and lay it on the table." Hewson complied, sweat breaking out afresh over his body.

"What's your name, doctor?"

"Hewson, Nigel Hewson."

"Well, Hewson, it seems you are carrying a miniature microphone hidden in the vent of your jacket. At least I suspect it is one. Where are the others?"

"Others?" He watched fascinated as Mornay crushed the microphone beneath his heel.

"Doctor, it is possible that you carried this bug unwittingly, but I suspect not."

At that moment Kuchinsky groaned and both men turned. Kuchinsky lay on the couch, his hands bound in front of him, but his feet free.

"There is your patient, doctor. Check him over."

Hewson knelt beside the semi-conscious form and pulled each eyelid open in turn. He rose and saw that Mornay stood between him and the emergency case. Muttering, "Excuse me," and praying inwardly, he stretched out his hand, closing it firmly around the handle. Mornay moved away, his face impassive, the pistol still pointed at the doctor who had begun to work on the stricken Russian. Hewson placed his stethoscope against the Russian's chest and listened intently. The heartbeat was ragged and irregular. "What exactly happened?" he asked, without looking up.

"Tell him, Al-Azhar. You seem to know all about Kuchinsky's illness," Mornay offered drily.

"He has angina, doctor, and carries nitroglycerine tablets. He took some the day before yesterday in Ottawa, that's how I know." The Sudanese diplomat sat upright. "How bad is it?"

Hewson continued to press his stethoscope to Kuchinsky's chest, finally rocking back and removing the stethoscope from his ears. "He has a very rapid beat with an unusual murmur. He needs immediate hospitalisation, oxygen and proper treatment."

"Not a chance, doctor. You both stay here."

Hewson spread his hands. He had not expected any other answer. "As you wish, but I must warn you he is in very poor condition and could go at any time."

"If he dies, it will be murder," Mike Monroe interjected, "and the government will treat it as such, believe me."

"Have mercy, Mornay, let him go," Al-Azhar broke in. "It will not serve your purpose to have him die."

Khufra said nothing while Yassin watched the drama with an ironic smile on his face: let them fight. Mornay stared at them all coldly, his eyes glittering.

"My daughter is still being held. Whether he lives or dies depends on the speed with which they release her. Understand this; if he dies, it will not lessen my determination to destroy you all if she is harmed."

The smile left Yassin's face and, for the first time, he felt real fear. The man facing them was no longer rational, despite the flat even tone of his voice. Yassin looked over at Ali Khufra and their eyes met. Nothing registered on the swarthy face, yet Yassin had the curious sensation that Khufra was concerned about Kuchinsky's illness.

In the communications cabin, Benson, McUlroy and Nichols strained to hear the faint sounds of conversation coming from the microphone hidden in the handle of the emergency kit. Despite its being the latest stealth technology available, with incredible clarity, nothing could degrade the quality of sound faster than being installed the wrong way round and then taped over with plastic tape. When Mornay had discovered the first microphone hidden in Hewson's jacket, the tension in the cabin had been electric. Nichols prayed that his guess about Mornay's reaction had been correct, but, even so, he could not dispel his fear at the thought of hearing a shot as Mornay executed Hewson as a warning. The reasonably mild reaction to the first bug caused them all to relax, but Mornay's last statement about not releasing Kuchinsky left no doubt in anyone's mind that he still held the advantage.

Benson turned to McUlroy and Nichols, "The ER teams are

on their way and it looks like we're going to have to risk an all-out assault. Mornay sounds determined and I'm sure that he means what he says; it also sounds as if Kuchinsky is seriously ill."

McUlroy massaged his knuckles; "What's the latest from the 747 on that island?"

Nichols reached out his hand and was given a computer printout by the communications sergeant. He scanned it quickly. "Ilha do Sal, nothing, except, as we know, they delayed the deadline for executing passengers but have now set a new one for dawn their local time. It does seem as if Mornay's action has stayed their hand for the moment, but it says they're now demanding actual proof that the delegates from PLO/Hamas are being held."

"What!" McUlroy and Benson were stunned: "Do those jerks think we staged this?" McUlroy pulled a battered pipe from his pocket, looked at it longingly, then replaced it in the same pocket. "Can you patch Mornay's telephone to the Satlink and download to Sal, if we can get him to allow one of the delegates to speak?"

"Yes, sir, we're working on that right now." The comm-sergeant was proud of his abilities.

"Bob, connect to the room again and tell him what the hijackers want. Explain that this might be the break we all need. Keep him talking for as long as you can."

Benson broke in, frowning: "And what if the delegates refuse to talk to the hijackers? It might make the situation worse. If the men on the 747 are paranoid enough to think that we're staging this hostage taking, they might react by shooting a few passengers in anger."

"Ken, let's take one step at a time. The ER team is not due for a while yet, so let's try a little strategy." McUlroy pulled the empty pipe out of his pocket and pointed the stem at Nichols. "Try again, Bob; he may have reconnected the jack by now." Nichols flipped a toggle switch and smiled, "It's ringing."

"Give it to me." McUlroy held out his hand.

In the hotel room everyone jumped as the telephone began

to ring. Mornay's hand shot instinctively to the bomb and Hewson noted the tightening of the muscles around the jaw. Mornay's eyes were unnaturally bright and the doctor guessed he was on a stimulant to stay awake. The prolonged effects of tiredness, tension and grief were beginning to take their toll. His eyes not leaving the group, Mornay picked up the receiver.

"Mr. Mornay?"

David waited without answering, frowning slightly.

"Mr. Mornay, my name is McUlroy, Inspector Nichols' superior. We have just been advised that the 747 hijackers are demanding proof that you are, in fact, holding the peace-conference delegates hostage. If you would release one of the delegates, you have my word that we will have him talk to the hijackers via a special line we are setting up. We also have several reporters from the major stations outside, so the coverage would be worldwide and leave no room for doubt."

"McUlroy, you can advise the hijackers that my conditions still stand. I will have one of the delegates talk from this room. You can arrange a direct link to the 747."

"That will not have the same effect, Mr. Mornay," but McUlroy spoke into a dead telephone. "Well, you heard him! Bob, send a message to the 747 that we're negotiating to have a delegate speak to them. Explain that we hope for it to happen shortly."

"Think it will work, sir?" Bob Nichols scribbled a message on the fax pad before keying the microphone on the metal table.

"I don't know. There's something very queer about this whole affair. Why are the hijackers so concerned for the delegates? First reports indicated that they were a splinter group and not part of the mainstream Hamas' organisation." He sucked at his unlit pipe. "Keep checking that connection every few minutes. I need to talk to Mornay again."

Chapter 18

Washington

The president of the United States stretched wearily. "Go on, Ed; what's the latest news?"

Ed Mason felt sorry for the man facing him. This was just one of dozens of problems that the president had to face every day. Dear God, how could any one human handle the workload, he wondered, but then his own workload was not too shabby, he thought wryly.

"Well, sir, it seems Mornay has given the hijackers pause. According to our link with the 747 there have been no more executions, although an hour ago they had Eli Natan call Tel Aviv."

"Yes, I know. Benjamin Mir called, and their cabinet is arguing over the possibility of releasing some of the Hamas politicals, but no one wants to even consider the hard cases."

"They won't accept that." Mason shook his head in despair. "Hell, these boys didn't hijack a 747 and penetrate the Mossad security in Washington just to get some politicals back."

"I know, and by the time they finally agree that it's important to keep Natan from spilling his guts, we're going to have a lot of dead people on the ground, including CANCEL. What's the status on the assault team?"

Mason looked at his watch and made a swift calculation. "Right now the Portuguese commandos are airborne and should hit the airfield two hours before the deadline."

"How good are they? Couldn't we have waited for the Rangers and Seals to position?"

Mason dragged both hands down his cheeks before answering. God, he was tired, and the answers seemed harder to find. "They're an unknown quality. The Brits know the colonel-in-charge and rate him highly. He and some of the others went through the SAS course at Hereford. As for the others, we just don't know." He looked straight at the president. "When we took the decision to assault the island, we assumed that the executions were imminent. As you know, our capability worldwide has been cut back and we had to assemble our own assault team here, so the short answer is 'no,' we cannot wait for the Rangers to position."

The president smiled grimly. Every day it seemed as if the rush to downsize the military had been too rapid and the much-vaunted peace dividend was just as ephemeral as any other form of government saving. "Don't belabour the obvious, Ed," he yawned. "What about the Canadians? Are they having any success in getting to Mornay?"

"No, thank God. The longer he acts as the wild card, the better our chances of cleaning this up. If the assault fails, he still has the delegates as a last-bargaining chip."

"You're getting far too cynical, my friend. What about Chernomyrdin? Is he still on track to visit the game reserve?" The president locked his fingers together, then inverted them and stretched, trying to work the knots out of his shoulders.

Ed Mason looked over at Jack Dehenny: "Jack?"

Jack Dehenny removed a file from the slim attaché case on his lap and drew out a tearsheet. "Last night, President Mandela thanked Russia for its help during the long struggle to defeat apartheid and awarded Vice-President Chernomyrdin the order of the Star of South Africa. He announced . . ."

"I'll bet Chernomyrdin is happy to be getting some good press coverage for a change." The president's tone was envious. It was an open secret that the American Presidency had troubles of its own, "Sorry Jack. I was thinking aloud . . . go ahead."

Dehenny smiled, for the apology had been swift and sincere. It was one of this president's biggest assets, his ability to treat people with consideration even over something as trivial as an interruption. "No sweat, sir. President Mandela, as expected, has arranged a visit for Chernomyrdin to the Kruger Park Game Reserve and then to take a private hunting trip to the Quazi restricted hunting zone."

"The long gun in place?" This time Dehenny smiled inwardly.

The president's term for the world-class marksman was as obsolete as James Bond.

"As of yesterday: perfect cover, and the extraction team posing as journalists are ready to move."

"How long before . . .?"

"If the assault team can have Espargos under control by 0700 hrs, the 747 can be refuelled and on its way to South Africa by 0900. As one of the regular passengers, CANCEL will have at least 12 hours to get to Quazi without arousing any suspicion and be in position in good time. If the SAA plane is damaged in the firefight, which is probable despite the use of RH weapons, we have dispatched as backup a SAC 747. It will pick up the passengers as soon as the airfield is secure and fly them on to South Africa. CANCEL will follow the usual procedures any hijacked passenger does: phone call home, etcetera." He paused for breath. "We're still going to pull this off, sir."

The jowly face came down slowly, the tired eyes focussing on Dehenny's face. In a voice that was little above a whisper: "We cannot fail, Jack; we must not." He hesitated, as if to add something, then waved his hand: "No, . . let's try to get some sleep. It's all in God's hands now. Ed, you will call me as soon as the assault team . . ."

"Of course, sir." They both knew what he meant. Assault teams had failed in the past. Both men rose in concert with the president and waited for him to leave, noting how his shoulders drooped as he walked away.

****

Empress Hotel – Victoria.

Hewson broke the silence. "Mr. Mornay, this man is dying. If I can carry him out on my back, he might have a chance." Looking at Mornay, Hewson realised that the man was totally detached from the plight of the sick Russian and only his over bright-eyes gave some semblance of emotion to his tired face.

Mornay looked at Hewson then at the semi-conscious Kuchinsky. "No, doctor," he spoke slowly; "the hijackers killed two female cabin crew simply to prove that they were serious. If I let you leave with Kuchinsky, it will be taken as a sign of weakness and so strengthen their resolve."

Shocked at the cold logic of Mornay's argument, Hewson snapped, "For God's sake, man, you can't play mind games with people's lives! None of the people here has harmed you."

"Be quiet, doctor!" The voice was harsh. "Like most of your generation you are totally ignorant of issues outside your own narrow environment. If you read more than the medical journals, you might be better inf . . ."

Like an uncoiling spring, Mike Monroe launched himself across the 15 feet that separated him from where David Mornay sat on the edge of a table. He had spent the last two hours carefully scraping the nylon cord against a steel edge of the coffee table behind his back. Whenever Mornay had looked in his direction, he'd frozen in anticipation of imminent discovery, for he was certain the glittering eyes had noted his surreptitious movements. But each time Mornay looked away, he calmed his racing heart and continued his slow, relentless scraping, feeling perspiration trickle down his arms. Finally his persistence paid off; the cord parted and, by carefully pulling, he disentangled the knot and removed the bonds from his wrists. He spent another 20 minutes carefully untying his ankles during periods when Mornay was preoccupied, first with McUlroy and then with Dr. Hewson.

Monroe had felt savage anger at being hogtied like some rodeo calf by this damned screwball, and the added humiliation of being treated with contempt was more than he could stand. Until this event, Mike Monroe's life had been one long unbroken run of success. Born into an upper-middle-class Toronto family, he'd been educated at Canada's top schools and read law at Queen's University. Good looking, athletic and charming, his long-term plan was elegantly simple: first learn government from the inside before stepping into the political arena, eventually to capture the top job of all. Predictably, Monroe had chosen a career in Canada's Foreign Service, and his now-separated wife could bitterly attest to an overweening ambition that often kept him late at work. His career had moved further and faster up the ladder than his peers who, despite their envy, grudgingly accepted that his was an exceptional talent. Lying in a corner, his wrists and ankles bound for hour after weary hour, Monroe had had time to reflect on the vagaries of fate and to contemplate how an event that should have been a diplomatic triumph would now probably end his career. He had watched, waiting for Mornay to move away from the camera bag, and was finally rewarded when Hewson distracted Mornay. He had never been seriously tested and often wondered if he had physical courage, yet now, at the moment of action, he felt nothing but a sharp excitement rather than the fear he had half expected. In a driving football tackle, he catapulted his 200 pound frame at Mornay with both arms extended in front of his body and was halfway across the intervening space before Mornay began to turn,

"Get him, doctor," Dar Yassin yelled, realising almost as soon as Mornay, the implications of Monroe's move.

Hewson was stunned by the turn of events and watched in amazement as Monroe, his legs weakened by long-binding and restricted circulation, began to fall. The force of Monroe's initial spring was such that his fingers actually grasped Mornay's jacket before he crashed to the floor at David's feet. Hewson hesitated before jumping to his feet and, in that moment, David Mornay trembling with shock, the tic in his cheek jerking like a demented puppet, was back in command. The Walther covered both Hewson and Monroe. David had not moved from his seat at the table and now he motioned Hewson back down to the floor, using the ugly muzzle as a pointer. Monroe rolled over onto his back and tried to sit up. He felt sick with disappointment at the failure of his legs and the fool of a doctor for not exploiting the situation. Feeling nauseous from the adrenaline released into his system and slightly dazed from banging his head on the edge of the table, he did not see Mornay's hand move. The pistol slammed against his temple, dropping him into total darkness.

"Be very careful, doctor; your life is on a thread."

Hewson licked his lips; his mouth was totally dry. Clearing his throat, he tried to speak but nothing except a strangled gasp came out. Satisfied, Mornay pointed at the bound delegates.

"Turn each of these men over, one at a time; I want to check their bonds, so stay ahead of me at all times—understood?"

Hewson nodded jerkily. He started with Al-Azhar, rolling him over, before moving backwards on his haunches to Dar Yassin and repeating the process without taking his eyes off Mornay.

In the communications cabin, the policemen stood silent. Yassin's yell to Hewson had cracked out of the overhead speakers. Seconds later, the murmur of Mornay's tight over-controlled voice told them that, whatever the attempt, it had failed. Nichols broke the silence: "Perhaps one of the shooters on the roof saw something. I'll check." He pulled the microphone over. "Knight, do you read?" There was silence for several seconds then, as he reached to transmit again,

"Yes, sir. Knight here."

"We've just had an indication that something happened in the room. Did you notice anything through the gap?"

"No, sir, there has been no change at all. The viewing area is small and someone, who I assume is Mornay, crosses the area occasionally but is not there long enough to give me a positive ID."

"Then nothing has moved across your view in the last few minutes?"

"No, sir. The area I can see has been empty for the last half hour."

Benson ran a hand through his thinning hair. "What orders have you given your sharpshooters, Bob?"

"The usual, sir: no execution without a direct order. I wanted to get a feel for the situation before taking the leashes off."

"You say that Knight can actually see into the room?"

"Yes, but it's not as good as it sounds. A window is slightly open and, from his position, Knight can see into the room an area about three feet square. Whoever passes through the area does not stop, so a positive ID is impossible."

"All the delegates are bound, aren't they? So it stands to reason that the only person who has freedom of movement is Mornay. I think," McUlroy tapped his pipe against his teeth reflectively, "that you should give Knight authority to fire at his own discretion. If the glimpses are as fleeting as you say, he will not have time to call for permission. I assume he has seen a picture of Mornay?"

"Yes, sir." Nichols felt his neck flush in anger. You don't put a man in a position to kill without the most thorough briefing. He snapped a toggle switch down. "Knight, do you read?"

"Go ahead, Firedancer."

"You are authorised to fire at your own discretion, but ensure positive identification of target."

They all heard Knight's sharp intake of breath. "Roger-Roger, Firedancer, I will fire only on positive ID."

"That's affirmative, Knight—Firedancer out." He snapped the button to 'off' and swivelled to face the other two. "It's one hell of a long shot." His tone made it clear that he was not happy with the decision.

McUlroy did not answer for a minute. "You were thinking of the doctor when you told him to fire only on a positive ID?"

"Yes. It occurred to me that Hewson might be moving around the room attending to patients." Nichols didn't add that shooting the doctor by accident would have been a catastrophe almost as bad as merely wounding Mornay and giving him time to activate his device.

McUlroy studied the face of his subordinate calmly. "It was a wise call," he smiled grimly. "Now, when the SWAT team gets here, have them position two men on ropes outside the window so that if Knight sees something, we at least have an approximate position to focus an attack on. Have the rest inside ready to rush the door. When is the SWAT team due?"

"Anytime now, sir."

While McUlroy and Nichols had been speaking, the overhead speakers were silent, and later Benson would confess to a feeling of despair that this event was going to end badly.

Above their heads, Mornay was methodically checking their bonds after Hewson rolled each man over. Only Khufra offered resistance, throwing his body about and frustrating the doctor's attempts to roll him over. Mornay looked up from checking Professor Watson's bonds and was about to speak when Dassin snapped an angry command at Khufra who stiffened as if slapped, then offered no further resistance.

"Ja, das wirt den Kampf vekürsen," his face slick with perspiration, Kuchinsky spoke in clear loud German. "Ein Unterseeboot ist würde die Antwort sein. . . ." The rest was unintelligible, and faded as he jerked spasmodically.

"Viktor, horst du mich?" All eyes snapped to the speaker Ali Al-Azhar who was struggling to get to his feet. "Kamerad, antworte mir. Kannst du mich hören?"

Mornay covered with a half-dozen strides the space to where Al-Azhar was forcing himself upright. He swung his open hand hard across his face, swinging the pistol within half an inch of the Sudanese diplomat's eye. "So, you speak German, and your friendly Russian is talking of submarines and winning the war. That wouldn't be the conflict with Israel, now would it?"

Al-Azhar, eyes bright with tears from the impact of the blow, snapped back harshly: "Yes, I speak German—also Spanish, French and English. He is my colleague and friend and he is dying because of your neglect. I have no idea what he is talking about."

"You lie. You know a lot more about the hijacking than I had thought." He paused, the hard grey eyes locked with Al-Azhar's. "I should have guessed. Khufra and Kuchinsky I suspected, but now it makes more sense. You bastards organised the hijack to get your Hamas comrades free. A submarine must have taken another group of hijackers to Ilha do Sal." His voice had dropped to a whisper; everyone sat silent, mesmerised by the unfolding drama. Outside in the communications shack, the three policemen strained to hear.

"That's it; that must be it. You planned to blow up the plane with all the passengers once your people were free, and the hijackers would disappear from Ilha do Sal by submarine." The feverish light in his eyes and the tic in his cheek were back. It was obvious to all watching that Mornay's icy self-control was breaking. "You grubby little thugs! What had you planned? . . . to let the aircraft take off with a bomb on board and disappear over the ocean or blow them up on the ground?" Mornay's rage was building and his voice rose with anger. "So that's why your friends on Sal want proof. . . . They'll get their proof, oh yes, they'll get their proof . . . Doctor, connect the telephone; it's time we ended this charade."

"I will not speak." The Sudanese diplomat's voice was firm. "I will do nothing to assist your wild speculations."

"Oh, yes, you will, Al-Azhar. Doctor, drag him over here."

Totally confused by what he had just heard, Hewson stepped over Monroe, not noticing a slight stirring. He placed his hands under Al-Azhar's armpits and dragged him over to the telephone table.

"Untie Khufra's feet; he's too heavy for you to drag here."

Hewson knelt beside Kuchinsky's still form and mopped the wet face with a moistened wipe he had taken from the open medical kit. He ignored Mornay's order and reached for a hypodermic, holding the needle up to the light and tapping it slightly to dislodge any bubbles. "I think he's nearly gone." He rolled up the Russian's sleeve and injected directly into the vein. After his delirious outburst, Kuchinsky had slid back into unconsciousness, and Hewson felt helpless, convinced that Kuchinsky was slipping into a terminal coma and fearing there was nothing further he could do for the man. He appealed to Mornay: "Can you at least ask for oxygen to be sent up?"

Mornay shook his head in disbelief at the doctor's question. "I said untie Khufra's feet, doctor, and leave the Russian alone."

"This man is dying. If I can get oxygen it might save him." He stared at Mornay beseechingly, his hands lifted in desperation.

"Doctor, I don't give a damn if he dies or not, but if you want to help him then do as I say. Untie Khufra's feet and, when he has broadcast, it might change the situation."

Hewson choked back a reply and walked over to where Khufra sat. Had his eyes not been so blurred with tears of frustration, he might have avoided the kick that Khufra aimed at his chest with both bound feet. The blow took Hewson by surprise and, with a startled grunt, he fell backwards into Professor Maxwell. Khufra spat a string of Arabic at the two men but was interrupted and cut short by a sharp command by Dar Yassin: "Enough, commander. The doctor is not your enemy."

"He is, he is . . . ," the burly Arab struggled with his English. "He is helping the Zionist dog." The veins in his neck stood out like knotted rope and his face was suffused with rage.

Mornay walked over, coming from the side to avoid a repetition of the kick Hewson had received. Khufra waited, no fear showing in his eyes. Had the man's arms been free, gun or no gun, David Mornay would have been in serious trouble. Mornay studied the Hamas field chief. Why was the Arab so determined not to speak to the hijackers of the 747?

"So tell me, you miserable excuse for a man, tell me why you think you will not talk if I wish you to?" The tic in his cheek was more pronounced than ever and his face was chalk white. While no one else in the room except the aides nearest Khufra heard the words, the intent on Mornay's face was chillingly clear. Hewson croaked out from the floor: "No, please! I'm OK, just winded." Mornay ignored him, and the Walther ripped down both sides of Kufra's face. Blood burst from the cuts. Reversing the pistol, Mornay slammed it again and again alongside Khufra's ears. He straightened, leaving the dazed Khufra to spit blood on to the carpet.

"Bring him to the telephone, Hewson. He has a call to make."

The Sudanese spoke quietly. Perhaps more than anyone he realised how close to death they all were. "Mr. Mornay, you are mistaken. We are not guilty of the hijack. I believe you are a just man and I ask you to please consider that you could be wrong. Victor Kuchinsky was babbling, as people in delirium sometimes do. It meant nothing."

"Sorry, Al-Azhar, good try, but you're not convincing enough. A little while ago I heard a newsflash that a high-level Israeli called Eli Natan was on the aircraft." Mornay gave a tight smile as Al-Azhar's eyes widened. The diplomat had completely forgotten the small radio in Mornay's pocket. "And now that I have blocked them from executing more passengers by threatening all of you, they have forced him to call Tel Aviv to add pressure on Israel to release Khufra's thugs. I suppose you're going to tell me that is just a coincidence"

Al-Azhar did not answer. A chess aficionado, he realised that, while the game was far from over, he'd just lost his queen.

Mornay turned away to watch Hewson help the dazed Khufra over to the telephone. Khufra did not protest as Hewson sat him down in a chair and began to clean the cuts on his face.

Mornay picked up the telephone. "Nichols, I want a direct connection to the aircraft on Sal."

McUlroy answered: "Stand by, we are attempting to connect; it will take a few minutes. Can I speak to Dr. Hewson?"

"Hewson is fine, no one is dead yet, but someone will be dead very soon if this line is not connected quickly."

Nichols pulled McUlroy's arm and nodded. "Your connection is established, speak up, for the line is poor."

Mornay pressed the telephone to his ear, static crackling like frying bacon. Suddenly the static stopped and he heard, " . . .Hullo, hullo Victoria, this is Ilha do Sal. Do you hear me, Victoria?"

"Who is speaking?"

"Victoria, this is Captain Strydom of South African Airways. Please speak louder, you are faint, about strength three."

"Captain, tell the leader of the hijackers to come to the mike."

"He is here; wait please . . ." A burst of static, more sounds like frying bacon then, ". . . is Colonel Davis of the 24th November Group. Go ahead."

"Davis, you wished for proof. Ali Khufra will speak to you, but first my daughter and Colin will speak to me—fetch her." The command was barked out.

David heard the captain come on again. "Wait please; Miss Mornay is coming." Something incomprehensible then, as Mornay swept his eyes over the room, "Daddy, is that you? Oh, daddy, Colin says . . ." The voice was cut off, then Davis spoke. "You have heard your daughter, and your nephew is standing by. Let Commander Khufra speak."

Mornay pushed the telephone over to where Khufra sat. For a second he seemed unaware that Khufra was still bound then, with a grunt, placed the receiver over the Arab's ear. He jammed the muzzle of the pistol hard into Khufra's groin. "Speak to your comrades, dog. Tell them to release the passengers or in five seconds you become a woman."

No one spoke. All eyes were on Khufra as he sat slumped in the chair, the adhesive bandages glaringly white against his swarthy skin. He was not as dazed as he pretended and he knew that if he pleaded with the hijackers all the credibility he had won over the years would be lost. Too often his fighters had seen him punish those who had shown fear in battle with the Israelis and demand that they accept a martyr's death rather than surrender. Now, to save his own skin he must ask them to surrender their hard-won prize. No, he told himself, he was not afraid and he still did not believe the Canadian had the nerve to kill. A harder man would not have allowed the doctor to come into the room. As he raised his swollen battered face, the mouth pulling into a snarl of defiance and contempt, his eyes widened as he saw Monroe crouching for a spring.

Slowly regaining consciousness, Monroe had lain still in the hope that another chance would arise. He could not believe that his arms and legs had been left free. Now all eyes, including Mornay's, were intent on Ali Khufra. Carefully, inch by inch, he moved his body into position for another attempt, gathering all his strength for one bound.

Mornay saw the look on Khufra's face the instant Monroe leaped, but this time the Canadian diplomat judged the distance to perfection. Another second would have had him on Mornay's back, but Khufra's face denied him that precious second. Mornay swivelled around but the Walther caught in the crotch of Khufra's lightweight wool trousers, and that condemned Monroe. He might have suffered nothing more than another blow to the head but now, in panic, Mornay had no time. He ripped the pistol free and fired into the bulky mass that was nearly on top of him.

The impact of the 9 mm, full-metal-jacket bullet slammed Monroe sideways. Travelling at 1,150 feet per second, the 115 grain lead-and-steel projectile entered Monroe's body in the Trapezius muscle that covers the shoulder area and ripped downwards through the entire length of his torso from shoulder to pelvis, smashing bone and ripping tissue before lodging against the left hip joint. Monroe was unconscious before he hit the floor. The roar of the unsilenced pistol in the confines of the room died away and, like frozen statues, no one moved.

Mornay, his cheek twitching uncontrollably, picked up the telephone from the floor. He seemed as stunned as the rest of them but he was still in command of the room, as the steady muzzle of the pistol indicated.

"Davis, Davis are you there?"

"What the hell is going on?"

"Stand by. Khufra will talk to you now." Once again Mornay ground the telephone against Khufra's ear, ignoring the man's wince of pain. Hewson rose from his knees, his hands in full view. He was scared, but he had noticed a slight movement in the still, bleeding figure lying at Mornay's feet and all his training drove him to ask, "Can I attend to Monroe?"

Mornay ignored him and spoke directly to Khufra. "OK, Khufra, this time you will talk. Tell them I will kill you, Yassin, and the others if the passengers are not released at once."

For all his cruelty, Khufra was of the Bedouin tribe and fear was not part of his people's character. But now, in the glittering mad eyes of the man facing him, he saw a rage such as he had not seen in a long time. An incident from his childhood flashed into his mind. He was putting sand into the eyes of a howling mongrel that had annoyed him when the refugee camp's diminutive Imam passed on his way to prayers. That day he learnt the strength that uncontrolled rage gives to men. Khufra remembered how his head had stung for days from the pounding he had received and now he saw the same rage.

"This is Commander Ali Khufra."

"Commander, are you held against your will?"

"It is true."

There was a long silence, then Kassim came on, speaking Arabic: "We will kill the passengers and keep the Zionist for interrogation."

Khufra weighed that for a moment: "No, release them."

"What of the Zionist spy?"

Khufra switched to English: "Take the aircraft to Beirut. Leave the passengers behind."

"But what of our brothers in the jails?"

Khufra, his face bruised and swollen, looked at Yassin who nodded. "You have achieved much. Be patient."

Mornay took the phone away from Khufra's ear. "Davis, do you hear me?"

"Yes, we have the message."

"When my nephew tells me that you have left Sal and that the passengers are safe, I will release all the delegates here."

"I understand. But you understand this, Mornay: we are taking the Israeli with us to guarantee no interference. He will be released with the captain and co-pilot at our destination." The line went dead.

Chapter 19

Washington

Jack Dehenny tore the sheet out of the high-speed fax. He read the first few lines and snapped to an assistant. "Get me the director and call the White House; we have to see the president again. Quick, man—move!"

Within 60 seconds an assistant handed Dehenny a phone. "Jeannie says the president is sleeping. How urgent is this?"

"Jeannie, it's a code amber. I'm sorry, but we must see him now." Dehenny waited for the connection to be broken then punched a series of numbers and made two further calls, his usually pleasant face becoming increasingly grim. He looked inquiringly at another assistant as he handed the phone back to a female officer. "Have you located the director?"

"Line 2, sir, the director's calling from his vehicle on the parkway." Dehenny again took the phone. "Ed, can you meet me at the White House? I'll wait at the South Entrance . . . No, not that, worse. It's a burst transmit from Topol and it's serious . . . Yes, I've called Jeannie and she's getting him up now." For a long moment Dehenny did nothing but stare at the pale cream wall of the communications room. His two assistants exchanged glances. Finally, the deputy director of the CIA turned to the nearest officer. "Lisa, I want you and Sam to stand by the machine and call me immediately anything comes in from Russia." He started for the door then paused and spoke over his shoulder. "Also anything on the hijack."

"Interrupt you even at the White House, sir?"

"Yes, of course. What do you think immediately means?"

Fifteen minutes later the two men met under the lights illuminating the door of the South Entrance. They stood in brief conversation before following the secret service agent down the long hallway into the Oval Office. "The president will be here presently." He moved back to stand against the wall, hands clasped across his stomach. The room was already occupied and, as the two CIA men entered, a tall, slim immaculately dressed man moved towards them. Dehenny noted sourly that not a silver-tipped hair on Roland de Courcy Hampton's head was out of place. The White House chief of staff did not smile, he was obviously not happy to have been dragged into this sudden meeting.

"What's all this about, Mason. Why is it so necessary to drag me into an unscheduled meeting at this hour?"

"All in good time, Rollie. I think you'll see why your presence is important." He turned back to Jack Dehenny. "Show me." Ed Mason's hand was outstretched. Jack Dehenny pulled the fax out of his briefcase and smoothed it before handing it over. Mason read the first few lines and looked up in astonishment. "How?—sweet Jesus—how?" He continued reading, flipping the fax over to read the attached second page. At that moment, the president walked through a panelled door, yawning.

"So," he rasped, "are we at war or something?" He motioned the three men to chairs, but Hampton remained standing, arms folded, every inch a patrician waiting for a report from the provinces of Rome. The two intelligence chiefs looked at each other, then Ed Mason spoke.

"We've had another message from Topol." He looked up at Hampton and his voice was neutral. "I have asked Rollie to sit in, Mr. President. There are important political considerations to the latest message."

The president frowned. "I hope you know what you're doing, Ed. You'd better brief him."

Mason hesitated, pushing his halfmoon glasses further up to the bridge of his nose.

"Within the Russian Parliament there's a group, code name Earthquake, that's intent on taking over Russia from Yeltsin. This group is comprised of old hardline communists and top military men who want to stop any further disintegration of what they consider the final borders. This group knows that they have no chance of succeeding with an old-fashioned coup. The Russian people, for a start, won't wear it. They have, therefore, developed a scheme to leave Yeltsin in place as a figurehead but remove Vice-President Chernomyrdin and other liberal reformist parliamentarians for people of their own beliefs. Chernomyrdin is the key. After his handling of the Chechnia crisis, he is widely respected. Their plan is to stage an accident while Chernomyrdin is at the Quazi Game Reserve in South Africa. We learned of this through a dissident inside the group. We don't know who he is and the whole point of sending CANCEL to South Africa was to keep Chernomyrdin alive while protecting our dissident as a source."

The chief of staff interrupted irritably. "Yes, yes—I'm fully aware of the political situation in Russia, and you seem to have forgotten that I sat in on the initial discussions when you planned to send an agent to South Africa." He turned to the President who looked up from the fax sheets Mason had given him to give his chief of staff a long, speculative look.

"Hear Ed out, Rollie. There's a lot you don't know, and it's important to keep some sort of sequence to events of the last two days."

Mason looked down to the notes in his lap and continued speaking in a flat, tightly controlled voice, his face devoid of all emotion,. "We know that a white supremacy group in South Africa called White Fire has been infiltrated by the Russian group. White Fire has been manipulated to attempt the assassination of President Mandela while he's showing Chernomyrdin the Quazi hunting area. They also have been led to believe that sympathisers from the ultra right in Germany and France are sending them a marksman who will kill Mandela. According to our source, the marksman is an ex-KGB specialist who has been reactivated. What the Whites don't realise is that the KGB man will fire the first shot close enough to Mandela to make it look like a near miss, probably taking out one of the security men. The second shot will kill Chernomyrdin and will be blamed on the shooter rushing his second shot at Mandela." He paused. "It's a very elegant play. The White supremacists get the blame; there's no linkage to Earthquake, and they can start rolling up the reformers one at a time. Our problem from the beginning was to protect our source, Topol, without putting Chernomyrdin in harm's way. If we alerted his security people, their precautions would immediately alert the Earthquake group that they had a leak and, no doubt, an intensive investigation would lead to Topol. We need Topol if we're going to neutralise the Earthquake group."

"And our man—what did you call him—CANCEL? He's to protect Chernomyrdin without letting the Earthquake group suspect . . . " Hampton had finally decided to sit and, pulling a chair around, faced Mason. "How are you going to do that?"

"Give the man a cigar." The distaste in Mason's voice permeated the room. "Got it in one, Rollie—except that CANCEL is a woman, not a man; a fact you weren't aware of, thank God."

"What on God's earth are you talking about?" Rollie Hampton stared at Mason. "Why in hell would that have meant anything to me?"

Mason extracted a piece of foolscap from his attaché case: "You're having an affair with this woman." Here he unclipped a 5"x8" photograph from the foolscap and held it up for Hampton to see. "Known to you as Helen Marchessa who works as a file clerk in the National Archives."

"What!" Hampton's mouth hung open in shock. "Do you mean to tell me that you've had me under surveillance? How dare you,—who gave you—under whose authority was this done?" Hampton's voice had risen sharply, and a fleck of spittle stuck to his upper lip. He looked at the president whose eyes were down, studying the fax: "Bill, did you know about this?"

"Let Ed finish." The president looked up, and his voice was icy cold.

Mason extracted a flat computer disk from his briefcase. "This is a record of all your conversations from the day the hijack started. Everyone who had even the most marginal information on CANCEL was put under full surveillance. We weren't interested in your cosy little affair, Rollie. If we fired every government employee who was cheating on his wife, Washington would be empty." He looked steadily at Rollie Hampton. "You weren't even a high priority for deep checking so your case was assigned to one of our junior staffers." He took a deep breath. "Thank God we're still getting high-calibre youngsters into the firm. Our young lady looked into your girlfriend's background, and everything seemed to be in order, but, cognisant of our fear that there was a highly placed mole, she backtracked through your girlfriend's past, mostly in her own time. She noticed that the lady drove way too fast in that little sports car you bought for her. Our agent checked with vehicle registry in Washington and noted that your friend had racked up a brace of speeding tickets in the Washington area; then our agent checked Seattle and Dallas, places where Ms Marchessa had resided previously and, surprise, surprise, they had no record of any vehicle infractions—not even a parking ticket. Considering her flamboyant driving style here, it didn't, as we say, 'flush clean.' The agent reported her findings to her superior officer and we turned the spotlight on your friend." As Mason bent over to place the CD back into his briefcase, the room was absolutely quiet: "Hence the microphone tap on your house and her apartment." Mason straightened up in the chair and, looking straight at Hampton, said softly, "It's our belief that you discussed highly confidential classified material with her."

His face still stiff with shock and outrage, Hampton had not moved while Mason was speaking, but, with the trained ear of the corporate lawyer he'd once been, he heard the magic words 'our belief' which must mean that Mason and the CIA were not certain. Obviously the tapes were not conclusive.

"I don't deny having an affair, but to suggest that I would discuss classified material is not only totally untrue but grossly offensive as well."

Mason shook his head slowly. "I know, you truly don't understand what you have done. You really are a vain and stupid man." Here Mason reached for the fax which the president passed him without breaking the awful silence that had descended. "Your girlfriend's real name is Helana Markova and she is a KGB asset inserted into the US before the change in the USSR. You see, Rollie, some of the old guard don't believe all the shit about a new world order. She was activated by her old boss who is now one of the Earthquake group and her task was to get close to you." Mason smiled thinly, without humour: "After all, your penchant for pretty bottoms is well known." His voice rose in sudden anger, "Haven't you learnt anything, anything at all?"

"Ed!" The president spoke sharply, "Keep to the facts."

"Yes, I'm sorry—When Eli Natan was on the hijacked SAA 747, we assumed that he was the target and offered the Israeli Embassy people assistance in tracking down their leak. After exhaustive checking, it became clear that they didn't have a leak so that left us with the possibility that we had been compromised. We ran covert close surveillance on all of our own people who might have had information on CANCEL'S mission and, as I said, found inconsistencies in the background of your little friend. Her cover was very, very good and might have escaped detection but for a determined young agent and, of course, we were running scared. Nothing holds up under that kind of scrutiny." Here Mason tapped his briefcase. "We also have recordings of everything you talked about when you were with her. It is now obvious that you were given to dropping hints about important events to impress your friend." He shook the fax at Hampton, his anger once again barely under control. "Our source, our precious source has confirmed that Earthquake knew we were sending an agent; they also knew the date and method of travel. Fortunately for us, when the hijackers saw Eli Natan they assumed he was CANCEL."

The president interrupted; "So they rigged the entire hijack with the express purpose of eliminating CANCEL?"

"Yes, sir, we are now certain that was the intent. They didn't know what CANCEL looked like so the whole plane was to be delayed until Chernomyrdin was killed. They knew that a rescue was pretty impossible from Sal. As usual, they wanted the biggest bang for their buck so decided to piggyback the Hamas agenda, wreck the PLO/Israel Accords, screw up our peace initiatives and, as an added bonus, get some of the Hamas radicals free. Of course, when they found Eli Natan on board they must have thought Allah was on their side for sure. We don't know why they felt it necessary to kill the two stewardesses but assume it was a pressure tactic to get the ball rolling with Israel. Our think tank feels the hijackers are probably Hamas fighters under the impression that their sole mission is to free the prisoners in Israel and that they probably know nothing of the Earthquake plan. We also think that the leader and several of his subordinates are either international terrorists or KGB specials." He breathed in deeply and turned to the ashen-faced chief of staff. "You, my friend, are in deeper shit than you can believe possible. I want . . ." He stopped, then turned to the secret service agent, "Take Mr. Hampton out. Have security lock him up and make sure he has no access to anyone or a telephone. I will want to speak to him again."

Roland Hampton rose to his feet, looking as if he had just heard a death sentence. He tried to speak, as he turned to the president, a friend of long-standing, but he saw only sadness and contempt in the president's eyes. Until the door closed behind the chief of staff and the secret service agent, no one spoke.

The president sighed. "It's my fault. Rollie has always been fond of the ladies but he's so damned good at his job that I made allowances. The damned fool could have cost us Topol. What's the prognosis? Can he survive in Earthquake after this?"

Ed Mason inclined his head at Jack Dehenny; "I'll let Jack tell you what our strategy is."

Jack Dehenny spoke quickly and concisely. "Our assumption, sir, is that Topol is not compromised, not yet. But if we're going to continue with our deception, we have to sacrifice Eli Natan."

"Explain." The hooded eyes never left his face, and Dehenny hated what he had to say.

"Mr. President, we propose letting Rollie return to his girlfriend and blurt out that Eli is our man. They are convinced anyway, and this will confirm that impression. Our computer simulations indicate that they will take Eli and a handful of passengers as hostages and fly to Beirut, leaving the bulk of the passengers at Sal. We will pick up the passengers and fly them on immediately to South Africa and have CANCEL continue with the plan."

"You are giving Eli Natan a death sentence. You know that, don't you?"

"Sir, they are going to kill him anyway. One of the Hamas, probably the leader, recognised him almost as soon as they landed at Sal. The only reason to let him go is if Israel frees the prisoners."

The president shivered. "And they wonder why we age so fast in this job. Yes . . . ?" A secret service agent had pushed open the door and was holding a hand up to his earphone.

"There's an urgent call for Mr. Dehenny, sir. Shall I have it put through?"

"Jack?"

"I told my staff to call me here if anything important came in from Russia or the hijack."

The president pushed a button on his desk, and a female voice spoke. "Sir, we have just had another intercept with the SAA aircraft and the man in Victoria."

Jack Dehenny leaned forward. "Play the tape, Lisa." There was a series of clicks and then . . ,

". . . This is Commander Ali Khufra."

"Commander, are you held against your will?"

"It is true."

There was a long silence, then someone speaking Arabic which had been translated: "We will kill the passengers and keep the Zionist for interrogation."

Khufra again. "No, release them."

"What of the Zionist spy?"

Khufra switched to English. "Take the aircraft to Beirut. Leave the passengers behind."

"But what of our brothers in the jails?"

Khufra again. "You have achieved much. Be patient."

A Canadian voice: "Davis, do you hear me?"

"Yes, we have the message."

"When my nephew tells me that you have left Sal and that the passengers are safe, I will release all the delegates here."

"I understand. But you understand this, Mornay, we are taking the Israeli with us to guarantee no interference. He will be released with the captain and co-pilot at our destination." The line went dead. . . .

For fully five seconds the three men sat stunned. Mason was the first to speak. "Holy Mother of God, he did it! He did it!" He seized Dehenny's arm in a vice-like grip. "It doesn't change anything. Hampton must still sow that disinformation." He turned to the president. "It can still work."

"What if they kill Eli Natan and then your plan works; surely they'll realise he wasn't CANCEL." The president obviously did not like the option presented.

"You remember, sir, that Rollie asked me how we were going to carry out the deception? Nothing as elegant as their plan, I'm afraid, but our counter force team decided that as CANCEL is one of our long-term assets, she was the best choice. She is part French, actually, very lovely and well known as a foreign correspondent for CNN." Mason grinned openly at the astonishment on the president's face."We've located the position the shooter will use. White supremacists are not particularly subtle; they've been making preparations for weeks. I'm amazed that South African Security haven't picked up on them. Christine is tasked to stick close to Chernomyrdin and, when the first shot comes, she will panic, knock him down, and fall on him until security gets into gear."

"You've got to be joking. Chernomyrdin must be 100 pounds heavier than she is."

"92 actually, Mr. President. She has a stun gun specially built into her bag. It has been field-tested and will knock Chernomyrdin flat in a second. The shooter will be allowed to escape and we will not block the extraction team. But we'll ensure the White Fire boys get their day in the sun."

"She'll brief Chernomyrdin?"

"Yes sir. After all the excitement has died down, she'll ask for a personal interview and give him what we know."

"OK, you have approval." The president levered himself tiredly to his feet. "Perhaps I can get a few more minutes in the sack. Oh yes, find out what the Canadians have planned for Moray . . ."

"Mornay sir, David Mornay."

"Mornay, yes—I don't want them to crucify him. We owe him, and it's time we paid some of our debt." The two men waited as the president walked to his private door. He stopped and turned and when he spoke it was with grim sadness: "Warn Rollie of the consequences if he fails to sow the disinformation convincingly. I will not have Eli Natan's blood wasted."

He did not wait for an answer and none was expected, but the two CIA men knew that they had also been warned.

Chapter 20

Victoria – Empress Hotel

Putting the phone down, Mornay sagged. He suddenly looked old and sick, and only the grim set of his jaw gave strength to the grey face.

Hewson looked up from his desperate ministrations on Monroe. "Mornay, this man is still alive. I need stretchers, oxygen and assistance. Please, you have won. Let me get these two men to hospital."

The Walther hung loosely in his hand as Mornay shook his head. "No, fix them up as best you can here. I will wait until I receive confirmation that my daughter is free."

"Mr. Mornay," it was Al-Azhar, "whatever you feel is your justification for holding us hostage, those two men are going to die, if the don't get help. As the doctor says, you have won. I beg you to reconsider."

"The Russian is your friend?"

"We have been colleagues a long time."

The pistol swung to point at Al-Azhar, and the look of bitter anger on Mornay's face sent a chill through the diplomat. "I should kill you now. You were part of this. Had my daughter been hurt . . ." He drew in a deep breath. "Damn you, damn you all . . . your miserable schemes for power, your bloody little backstreet plots . . . it's always the little people who suffer. What about the two young girls your hijacker friends killed? . . . You bloody excuse for a human being." The pistol centred on Al-Azhar's face as Mornay struggled to control his rage. He pointed a stiff finger at the Russian lying on the sofa. "So, he is your friend and you do not want to see him die. Well, that's too bad and a little late; you should have thought of the consequences before you played power games with the lives of innocent people."

The Sudanese paled beneath his dark tan and remained silent. Mornay turned to watch Hewson. "How bad is Monroe?"

Hewson finished putting a surgical dressing over the wound in Monroe's shoulder. "He is very bad. I suppose you think he is guilty of the hijacking as well," he added bitterly.

"No, Hewson; he is a brave man, but also a fool. The explosive in this case could remove the entire room." David looked around the room then picked up the telephone again. "Nichols?"

"Yes, go ahead, Mr. Mornay."

"As you have been listening in, you will know that the hijackers are going to release the passengers and that I will release the delegates as soon as I have confirmation from Sal. Send up two stretchers immediately. The doctor will accompany the injured out. I warn you not to attempt a forcible entry. Until I have confirmation, no one else leaves this room."

"We understand. Two stretchers are on their way up now, and they will be alone."

David walked slowly over to the window and pulled the heavy curtain back a few inches to peer down into the street below. Later, Hewson would say that he had never seen such tiredness in anyone and it was obvious that Mornay had stopped thinking clearly, or what happened next would not have occurred.

Lying on top of the Carillon Tower, Knight saw the curtain draw back and was stunned to see Mornay's profile staring down into the gardens below. His only communication was with the Comm. trailer and he'd not heard of the hijackers' capitulation. His last order from McUlroy had been to shoot on positive ID. He slid the Winchester up and pulled the scope into his right eye. Mornay's profile jumped into view and he centred the cross hairs on Mornay's temple. Ten minutes earlier the ERT team had arrived, and two of that team were now suspended on ropes on either side of the window. He knew the drill from dozens of gruelling hours of practice. He would drop the suspect, and simultaneously the ERT team would swing through the shattered window into the room. He breathed softly into his microphone, to warn the ERT team, 'target ID'd, stand ready,' and took up the first pressure on the trigger.

Below in the Comm. Trailer, Nichols wiped the perspiration

from his brow and spoke to McUlroy and Benson. "We had better stand down the ERT team. Mornay's voice profile still shows very high stress levels; any sudden moves on our part could still tip him over the edge." The two men signalled agreement, and Nichols pushed a key. "This is Firedancer to all units. No action; repeat, no actio . . ." A high-pitched squeal came from the overhead speaker as Knight's transmission clashed with Nichols . . . "Target ID'd stand ready."

"NO! . . . NO!" Nichols yelled into his microphone.

Johal Parminder had been the first member of his family to join the police force, and he remembered how his father had gripped his shoulders fiercely in a rush of pride the day he graduated from the police college. Then followed the long and difficult selection process to be included in the ERT team. Now, hanging outside the window, he was reaching for his winch switch when he heard Nichols' command. The sudden confusion and Nichols' desperate yell caused him to turn sideways to signal Knight, but the combination of reaching for the winch switch and turning towards Knight brought his leg into the same frame as Mornay's head. Knight jerked the rifle fractionally as Nichols' yell blasted into his headphones, but he had already taken up the final pressure and dispatched the bullet in one continuous movement.

Mornay spoke as the bullet, deflected by Knight's fractional jerk and then ripping through the tissues of Johal Parminder's leg, slammed into his chest, punching him back into the room.

Hewson said later that it sounded as if Mornay had been saying, "I kept my promise, Kate." Most of the others remembered only the window erupting inwards and Mornay flying backwards under the impact of the bullet. Within minutes the room was full of blue-uniformed police and medics. The long nightmare was over.

Chapter 21

Aftermath

Colin, Laura and the other passengers were shoved and prodded by the Hamas strike force to evacuate the hijacked 747 quickly. Reaching the concrete at the bottom of the boarding stairs, Colin saw an unconscious, badly beaten passenger dumped unceremoniously on the concrete. Stopping, he turned back and, ignoring the shouted instruction to wait for Khalil to reach the top of the ramp, lifted the slight, limp body. Running, with Laura trotting by his side, Colin carried his human cargo to the Sal airport terminal where a vacationing doctor stepped forward and immediately started work on the bloodied mass Colin laid on the table.

Colonel da Silva's men touched down on the airfield perimeter minutes after the 747, now empty of its former passengers and filled with the Hamas force, had climbed into the overcast sky, Captain Strydom controlling the aircraft while First Officer Des Bowen tended to the unconscious Eli Natan. Kassim had decided that if Natan was to be left alive he would at least carry some marks to express Hamas' anger. Davis had finally pulled Kassim clear with a curt 'enough!' Khalil had dragged the unconscious Israeli to the floor beside the cockpit bunk. Prior to take off, Captain Strydom had flatly refused to allow other crew members to remain on board despite several volunteering to remain at their posts. He had lost two of his crew and had no intention of losing more.

Fighters from the Principe de Asturias tracked the SAA 747 towards the coast of Mauritania, but no action was taken to force it down; there were the two crew members and the Israeli hostage to consider, and Captain Strydom had warned of an explosive package in the cockpit and threats by the hijackers to detonate it, if attacked.

Sweeping in over the flat coast, Da Silva's men jumped from the hovering helicopters and fanned across the airfield, searching for any remaining hijackers and hidden explosives. The colonel, running from the drop zone with his lead commando of ten men, raced to surround the terminal buildings. Satisfied that no diehard snipers were in the vicinity, he motioned two men up to the rooftop while he strode into the terminal to check on the passengers. The Portuguese colonel's eyes swept over the huddled passengers, most of whom were still numbed by their brush with death and unaware of the events that had led to their release. Da Silva saw Colin and the doctor working frantically.

"Are there any other injured?" He stared down at the injured man and, without waiting for an answer, snapped over his shoulder to his sergeant. "Get Timo and the medical equipment." The sergeant spun, and, as he ran for the door, Colin looked up from wiping blood off the injured man's face.

"I don't know; I didn't see anyone else in this condition. I heard that someone in the tourist section was pistol whipped and must be around here somewhere, but I haven't had time to check. They also murdered two stewardesses." Colin took a deep breath and found that his hands were shaking so hard that he dropped the torn shirt he was using to clean the injured man's face. He bent to recover the rag, but the little colonel stopped him.

"Leave it. My medical team will be here in a few minutes and they are trained to deal with these sorts of injuries." Da Silva was well acquainted with post-combat stress reaction and saw in the young man facing him the familiar signs. He gripped Colin's shoulder hard. "Steady—steady now—it will pass, and I need your help; come with me." Without waiting, the colonel turned and made for the main group of passengers gathered in the restaurant. Colin hesitated then, gratefully relinquishing responsibility, followed, leading Laura by the hand.

The colonel jumped up on to a table and raised his hands to command silence. "I am Colonel da Silva of the Portuguese Army. My men are busy securing the airfield and searching for any terrorists left behind. We were sent to secure your release but, for reasons that are not yet clear, events have changed quickly and precluded action on our part." He looked around the room. "Please identify anyone who needs medical attention. Do not, repeat, do not go outside the terminal until my men have completed their sweep; it is possible that explosives have been left behind. A 747 of the American Air Force is inbound and should be here shortly. Then you can continue your journey to South Africa."

A babble of voices rose, some protesting, but the colonel, ignoring the shouted calls, jumped down from the table. He gripped Colin's arm, "Follow me. I need information; perhaps you can help. We'll find a quiet room—ah—here we are." He pushed open a door and they found themselves in a small office. Closing the door, the colonel noticed Laura for the first time. "Your daughter?"

"No, she's my cousin." Colin shivered. "What happened? Why did they push us off the plane? Did they know you were coming?" He crossed both arms across his chest to control the shivering.

"Sit down." The colonel pulled a chair out; "You are suffering from reaction to high stress—it'll pass." He smiled kindly, "Believe me, I know." Colin relaxed slightly. This tough-looking soldier reminded him of Rafa. At that moment the door opened and a stocky soldier in camouflage battledress looked in. Turning, the colonel rapped out a string of commands in Portuguese. "I've told him to find you some hot sweet tea or, better yet, some brandy. Now, do you think you can answer some questions?

"Yes, of course,—what do you want to know?"

For the next 20 minutes, while he sipped tea laced with brandy, and Laura flipped over a magazine that had been found for her, Colin answered the colonel's rapid questions. He was particularly interested in the leaders of the hijack team, jotting down Colin's answers in a notebook pulled from a large pocket in his camouflage jacket. Puzzled by Colin's remark that Davis had said his uncle had held up a group of people in Canada, the colonel asked the sergeant to find a commercial radio. The sergeant was back in a few minutes with a worldband radio supplied by one of the passengers. They caught the tail end of the hourly BBC news.

"...*to repeat the headline news, the hijack of the SAA airliner with 300 people on board is over. NATO forces from Portugal are in charge of Ilha do Sal, arriving shortly after the hijackers, with one hostage and two flight crew had taken the commandeered aircraft in the direction of North Africa. It is assumed their eventual destination is Libya. The hostage taking in Victoria, British Columbia, of the PLO/Hamas delegation by a man believed to have a daughter on board the hijacked aircraft is also over. At the moment our information is incomplete and we will have a full report on the next news broadcast; however, it does appear that the man in Victoria—hold on, I've just been handed an update—the man, a Mr. David Mornay, has a nephew and daughter among the passengers. It does appear that Mr. Mornay's action caused the hijackers to abandon their attempt to free Islamic militants from Israeli jails. The next news broadcast will be in one hour."*

"You are the nephew?" Da Silva leant forward, his dark eyes boring into Colin.

"Yes . . . ," Colin seemed bemused; "that's my uncle Dave they're talking about." He started to grin and then suddenly was laughing aloud.

The colonel and the two soldiers in the little room were also grinning. The colonel nodded. "This uncle of yours must be an extraordinary man."

"Yes, he is; at least, I think so." Colin touched the colonel's machine pistol lying on the table. "He was once a soldier, like you. But in the American Marines, in Vietnam."

"I see." The colonel hesitated, then reached inside his open shirt, fumbling for a moment, and with a grunt, finding what he wanted, removed a thin chain from around his neck. He stood looking at the chain in his hand, knelt beside Laura, then hung the chain, to which was attached a small silver medallion, around her neck. Placing both hands on her shoulders, but looking at Colin, he spoke gravely. "This St. Christopher was given to me by my wife, many years ago, when I fought in Angola and Mozambique. Tell your uncle, from one soldier to another, that

I salute him." He brushed his lips to Laura's forehead. "And you, little one, may it protect you as it has protected me." He stood, brushed his knees and reached for the pistol. "Come, I hear your aircraft arriving."

———————————

In Israel, a plain, steel-sided grey police van was hurriedly recalled from Tel Aviv airport where an unmarked jet transport sat on the runway. The van's occupants were returned to the maximum security wing of the jail. Much later, a senior officer in the Canadian Security Intelligence Service would, after a particularly wild party, mention a deal between the Canadian and Israeli governments. Attempts by a newsman who overheard the comment to follow up were frustrated by bland denials in Tel Aviv and Ottawa.

In Victoria, public feeling was ambivalent. A poll taken by a local radio station showed a surprising number of people who wholeheartedly supported Mornay's conduct—after all, it had worked hadn't it? Most felt that the local and federal forces had done as much as could be expected under the circumstances. Benson and McUlroy received commendations for their conduct and were lionised on their return to Ottawa but, in the aftermath, Nichols slipped quietly back into his regular routine.

———————————

In Johannesburg, the grey US Air Force 747 landed the shaken-but-relieved passengers who were immediately surrounded by scores of news media and relatives. The first secretary from the Israeli Embassy pushed his way through the crowd to reach the small group of Israeli passengers who had been roughed up by the hijackers. While most had received nothing more than a slap or a punch, a South African Jewish businessman had been singled out for a particularly savage beating. Kassim had exploded with rage on finding documents in the man's briefcase linking him to the arms trade between the Israeli Defence Ministry and Armscor, the South African armaments industry. This was the man whom Colin had carried into the terminal at Ilha do Sal. The secretary watched as the man was unloaded by stretcher. He touched the businessman's hand gently, trying not to stare at the brutally smashed face swathed in bandages.

Now in Johannesburg, his shirt still blotched with patches of dried blood, Colin held Laura's hand and ignored the flashing cameras and screeching calls from reporters as he searched for Laura's grandparents, Trish and Jack Scott. He stood her on his shoulders, giving her a clear view and the photographers a shot that would grace the front pages of every morning newspaper in the Western World.

"Batchi," Laura yelled, tapping Colin on the top of his head. "I see Batchi." Following Laura's directions, Colin bulled his way through the crowd to where Jack Scott enfolded Laura in his arms and Trish hugged Colin, tears running down her face. Standing to one side, Rafa stood with Joel Buchinsky, the Mornay Industry's chief pilot. Nigel Mornay had dispatched the company jet to Johannesburg the moment the hijacking was over with strict instructions to return at once with Colin, Laura and the grandparents, if they were able to travel. Seeing Rafa, Colin gently broke free from Trish's embrace and gripped the stocky Chilean's arm. "Uncle Dave was shot? We heard that he was shot, but nothing else. Is he . . ?"

Rafa smiled, "Yes, he was shot but he will recover. He was very lucky. The bullet ricocheted off a policeman's leg and hit him in the chest instead of the head. Right now he is in Victoria General Hospital after surgery to remove the bullet and that old piece of shrapnel. I spoke to your father at the hospital an hour ago." He hugged Colin gently. "I hear that you did well, amigo." Seeing Colin's puzzled frown, he explained: "One of the people on the plane spoke to a reporter near us and praised your coolness."

Colin brushed the praise aside. "What will happen to Dave now? Are they going to charge him? What about the UN fellow he shot? Is he out of danger? Jesus, Rafa, he has committed a string of offences . . . You know what the Canadian government is like. They'll lock him up and throw away the key."

"Slow down, for Heaven's Sake! I'll tell you all about it on our way to Scottie's place, but it's not as bad as it seems. For some reason the Americans are supporting Dave and claim he must have been suffering from post-traumatic stress—what we used to call combat fatigue. They have released Dave's records to the Canadian government with, get this, a presidential recommendation for clemency. Your father has been in touch with the prime minister. Everything I have told you is still confidential, but it looks as if he will get off." He laughed at the look of relief on Colin's face. "So now you're his keeper, eh? Come, amigo, let's get the luggage and get you home."

The little group, arms linked around each other, made for the terminal doors and the sun-splashed parking area outside.

———————0———————

Epilogue

The SAA 747 thundered through the night sky high over the Gulf of Sirte. Captain Strydom tensed and relaxed his shoulders, stretching tired muscles and staring wearily through the windscreen while Des Bowen slept. They had taken turns flying the big jet on its long curving journey over Mauritania, Northern Mali and Tunisia, and now the lights of Tripoli were behind them as they slid over the dark Mediterranean on the final leg towards Beirut. An involuntary shiver passed through the big captain's frame. Ten minutes earlier he had gone back to check on the Israeli and, staring down at the desperately injured man, he wondered if the hijackers were going to keep their word.

"Lock on . . . I have Lock on."

"Roger, Striker One, we confirm lock on. Stand by . . ." The voice was

calm, unaccented. *"Striker One, you are cleared to arm weapons . . . Striker Two, confirm status."*

"Striker Two has target identified. Range, four kilometres . . . standing by."

The two matt grey fighters slid silently side-by-side through the sky behind and below the 747. No identification was visible on either aircraft and, apart from several highly improved versions of the American air-to-air Sidewinder missile, nothing indicated their country of origin.

"Striker One, you are authorized to execute judgement . . . Striker Two, you are authorized to complete judgement, if required after Striker One breakaway . . . confirm."

"Roger, Striker Two,"

"Roger, Striker One attacking now." Even the flat metallic hiss of the radio could not disguise the tremor in Striker One's voice. The pilot lifted his hand and pulled the anti-flash visor down over his night glasses. His gloved hand trembled slightly as he lifted the red safety cover beside his right knee. Moving his hand back to the stick, he centred the glowing green dot on his Head-Up-Display on the belly of the giant 747 where the wings crossed the fuselage.

Two glowing trails erupted from under Striker One's wings, the missiles streaked in converging lines to join as one under the belly of the doomed 747.

"Breakaway! . . . breakaway! . . . Striker One, launch complete." The pilot of Striker One, after launch, had heeled his fighter into a tight climbing turn to starboard, leaving Striker Two in position for the second attack.

Suddenly the night sky erupted into a massive fireball as the fuel in the belly tank of the 747 exploded, tearing the jumbo apart as if it were paper mache.

"Striker Two confirms judgement executed . . . catastrophic destruction." Hauling hard to port on his stick, the pilot of Striker Two felt a savage buffet on his aircraft as the shock wave slammed into his fighter. Then he was clear and climbing hard.

"Allah Akbar." The ground controller's voice was calm, unaccented.

There was no reply from the two fighter aircraft as they flew East toward the early morning sun away from the wreckage spiralling down into the sea.

---------------0---------------

if you have enjoyed reading **'To Taunt a Wounded Tiger'** you will also enjoy **'The East Wind,'** by the same author, the second printing due for release in April 2005. You may order your copy direct from the publisher.

A short excerpt from: THE EAST WIND by Anthony Bruce.

Colin
The beginning of the end

The boy had begun to die, unaware that his lifespan could now be measured in hours. For the first time an eddy of fear stirred in his belly. Again he stared over the shimmering stony plain to where the Chuosberge mountains stood blue in the distance.

Nothing moved, except an eagle, a black speck circling aimlessly against the inverted vitreous bowl that stretched cloudlessly from horizon to horizon.

. .

As yet he didn't feel very thirsty, though his body had begun to give up precious fluid to keep his vital organs cool; dehydration had started and despite the heat he shivered. A drop of perspiration rolled down his nose from the band of his safari hat. He tasted salt. "Good," he thought. What had Kresfeld said? Something about while there was still salt in the sweat there was a chance. Wishing that he had taken more notice of the old German's words, he tried to recall all that Kresfeld had said, but only the frightening statistics came to mind.

This was the Namib, the oldest desert on earth, known to the Bushmen, those tough hardy survivors from the Stone age, as the land God made in anger. Here time meant nothing. Here the incredible Welwitschia plant, a living fossil drawing moisture from the night mist, had been dated to centuries before the birth of Christ ... In the empty silence he could hear his own heartbeat. To hide the welling fear from himself, he began to scream curses against the father who had placed him in this position and the uncle who had done nothing to prevent its happening. Not even an echo came back to mock him, for the desert didn't care. Men had died here before and, if imprudent or unlucky, would do so in future.

Finally he fell silent, exhausted, and the tears came spilling over sunburnt cheeks to evaporate quickly in the hot dry air. More precious liquid was lost and his body died a little more.

Unimog growled along the canyon floor, its heavy duty, deep ribbed tires alternately gripping and spinning in the sand and gravel of the dry river bed. The continual change in traction jerked the three men sitting side-by-side in the open driving compartment like puppets on a string. The driver, a young man in khaki work clothes, mumbled an apology to his companions.

"Not your fault." The big man sitting next to the driver brushed a hand irritably across his massive black beard, forcing the myriad of flies to ascend, flies that were trying to drink the perspiration that trickled down his deeply tanned face and disappeared into and over the tangle of his beard. "This bloody place would be hard on a hovercraft." Another jolt brought a grunt from all the occupants and the big man closed his hand on the arm of the driver.

"Stop for a second, let Johnny have a look through the glasses."

The third man addressed as Johnny waited until the Unimog had stopped before climbing up onto the bench seat. He steadied himself with one hand on top of the windscreen while he swept the canyon ahead through high power binoculars for the object of their search. The other two waited, listless, the all pervading heat sapping their energy so that even talk was an effort. A puff of wind, blasted sand across the floor of the canyon and despite the heat the big man shivered.

"You see that? The East Wind is coming, by tomorrow night it will be here in full strength so let's find the bloody camp and get the hell out of here - any luck Johnny?" He looked up at the ....